NOV 1 5

ALSO BY VLADIMIR SOROKIN

Day of the Oprichnik

Ice Trilogy:
Bro
Ice
23,000

The Queue

THE
BLIZZARD

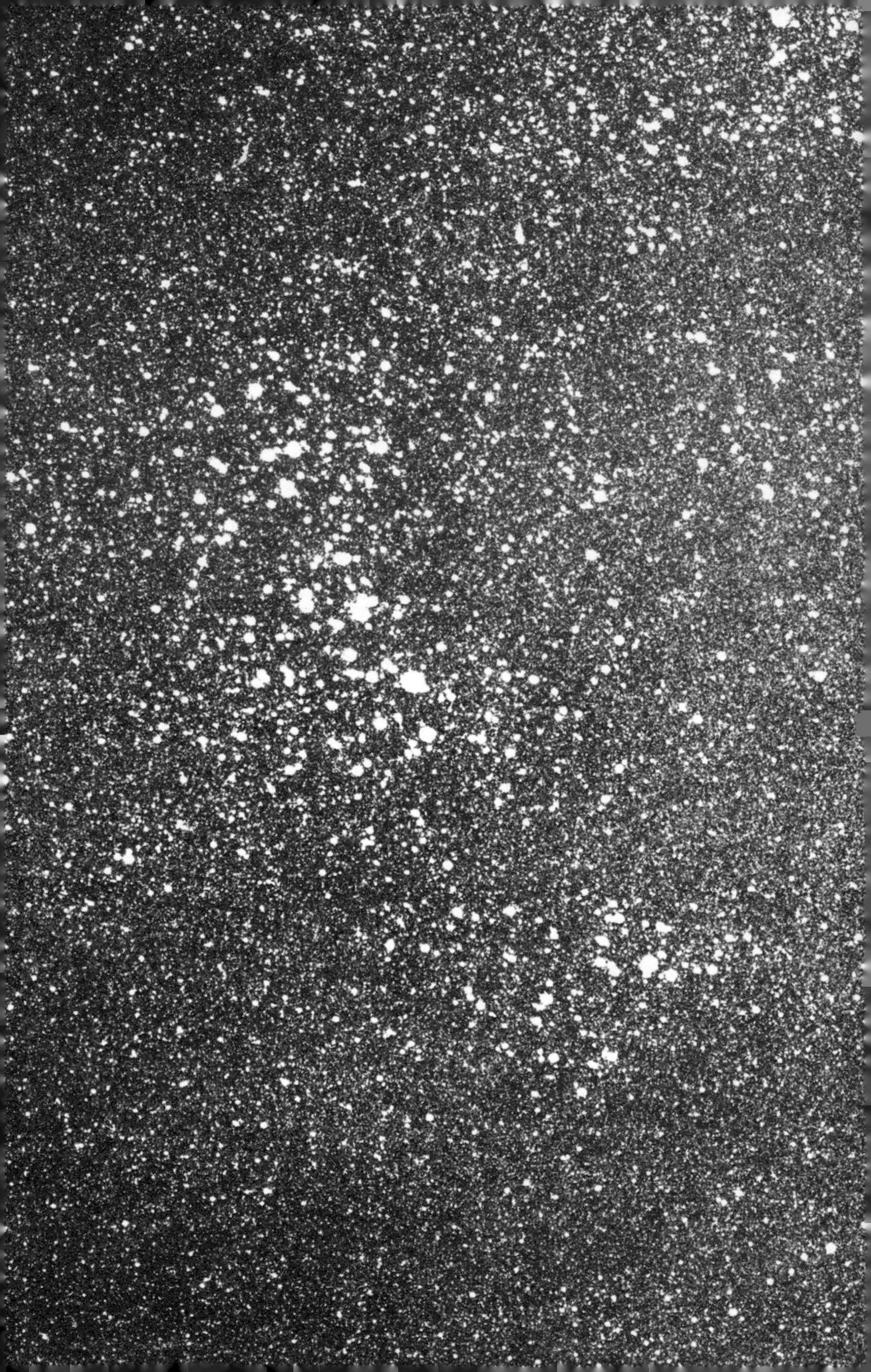

THE
BLIZZARD

———

VLADIMIR
SOROKIN

TRANSLATED FROM THE RUSSIAN BY

JAMEY GAMBRELL

FARRAR, STRAUS AND GIROUX

NEW YORK

Farrar, Straus and Giroux
18 West 18th Street, New York 10011

Library of Congress Cataloging-in-Publication Data
[Metel'. English]
The blizzard : a novel / Vladimir Sorokin ; translated by Jamey
Gambrell. — First American edition.
    pages   cm
Published in Russian under the title Метель.
ISBN 978-0-374-11437-4 (hardback) — ISBN 978-0-374-70939-6 (e-book)
    1. Dystopias—Fiction.   2. Psychological fiction.   I. Gambrell, Jamey,
translator.   II. Title.

PG3488.O66 M4813 2015
891.73'5—dc23   2015010964

Designed by Abby Kagan

Our books may be purchased in bulk for promotional, educational, or business use.
Please contact your local bookseller or the Macmillan Corporate and Premium
Sales Department at 1-800-221-7945, extension 5442, or by e-mail at
MacmillanSpecialMarkets@macmillan.com.

www.fsgbooks.com
www.twitter.com/fsgbooks • www.facebook.com/fsgbooks

1   3   5   7   9   10   8   6   4   2

Published with the support of the Mikhail Prokhorov Foundation TRANSCRIPT
Programme to Support Translations of Russian Literature

A dead man lies asleep,

Upon a bed of white,

Swirling at the window

Is a blizzard calm and light.

—ALEXANDER BLOK

THE
BLIZZARD

You have to understand, I simply must keep going!" Platon Ilich exclaimed angrily. "There are people waiting for me! They are *sick*. There's an *epidemic*! Don't you understand?!"

The stationmaster clenched his fists against his badger-fur vest, and leaned forward:

"Well now, whaddya mean, we don't understand? 'Course we do. You don't wanna stop, 'course I understand. But I don't got horses and ain't gonna get none till tomorrow!"

"What do you mean you don't have horses?!" Platon Ilich cried out in a livid voice. "What is your station for, then?"

"That's what for, but all of 'em are out, and there ain't a one to be found nowheres!" the stationmaster shouted, as though speaking to a deaf man. "Not 'less some miracle brings the mail horses in tonight. But who knows when they'll get here?"

Platon Ilich removed his pince-nez and stared at the stationmaster as though seeing him for the first time:

"My good fellow, do you comprehend that people are dying?"

The stationmaster unclenched his fists and stretched his hands toward the doctor like a beggar.

"Who don't understand dying? A'course we does. Good Russian Orthodox people dying, it's a terrible business. But look out the window!"

Platon Ilich put his pince-nez back on and automatically turned his puffy eyes toward the frost-covered windows through which nothing could be seen. Outside, the winter day was still overcast.

The doctor glanced at the clock, which was shaped like Baba

Yaga's hut on chicken legs; it ticked loudly and showed a quarter past two.

"It's already past two!" He indignantly shook his strong, close-cropped head, tinged with gray at the temples. "Past two o'clock! And it will get dark, don't you get it?"

"A'course, why wouldn't I be getting it—" the stationmaster began, but the doctor interrupted:

"I'll tell you what, old man! You get me some horses if you have to dig them up out of the ground! If I don't make it there today, I'll take you to court. For sabotage."

That familiar government word had a soporific effect on the stationmaster. He seemed to fall asleep, all his muttering and explaining coming to an abrupt halt. He wore a short vest, velour pants, and high white felt boots with yellow leather soles sewn on. His body was slightly bent at the waist; he seemed to freeze, remaining immobile in the dim light of the spacious, overheated chamber. On the other hand, his wife, who until now had been sitting quietly and knitting behind a calico curtain in the far corner, turned and peered out, showing her broad, expressionless face, which the doctor had already grown sick of over these last two hours of waiting, drinking tea with raspberry and plum jam and leafing through year-old copies of the magazine *Niva*:

"Mikhailych, what about asking Crouper?"

The stationmaster perked up immediately.

"Hmmm, we could try Crouper," he said, scratching his left arm, and half turning to his wife. "But they want official horses."

"I don't care what kind they are!" the doctor exclaimed. "Horses! Horses! I just want hor-r-r-ses!"

The stationmaster shuffled over to the high counter:

"If he ain't at his uncle's in Khoprov, we c'n try . . ."

He lifted the telephone receiver, turned the handle a couple of times, stood up straight, put his left hand on the small of his back, and raised his balding head high as if trying to grow taller:

"Mikholai Lukich, it's Mikhailych here. Tell me, our bread man passed your way this morning? No? All right then. A'course not! Not going nowhere now, not a chance . . . you're right. Well now, I'll be thanking you."

He replaced the receiver carefully. Signs of animation appeared on his carelessly shaven, ageless face, and he shuffled over to the doctor:

"Crouper didn't go to Khoprov for bread today. So he's here, prob'ly lying about next to the stove, 'cause when he goes to fetch bread, he always drops by his uncle's. They have a cup of tea and chat up a storm. He don't bring our bread till suppertime."

"He has horses?"

"He's got a sledmobile."

"A sledmobile?" The doctor frowned, taking out his cigarette case.

"If you beg him and explain, he'll take you to Dolgoye on his snow sled."

"And my horses?" Platon Ilich's forehead puckered, as he remembered his sleigh, driver, and pair of work-issued official horses.

"They can stay put for the time bein'. You can go back on 'em!"

The doctor lit up and exhaled smoke:

"And where is this bread man of yours?"

"Not too far aways from here." The stationmaster gestured behind him. "Vasya over there'll take you. Vasya!"

No one answered his call.

"He's like to be in the new cottage," the stationmaster's wife called out from somewhere behind the curtain.

She stood, her skirts swished across the floor, and she left the room. The doctor retrieved his heavy floor-length beaver coat from the coatrack, put it on, set a wide fox-fur hat with earflaps on his head, threw a long white scarf around his neck, pulled on his gloves, grabbed both of his traveling bags, and stepped firmly over the threshold of the door that the stationmaster had opened for him into the dark mudroom.

Platon Ilich Garin, the district doctor, was a tall, sturdy forty-two-year-old man with a long, narrow face and a large nose; he was closely shaven and always wore a look of concentrated dissatisfaction. His purposeful face, with its large, stubborn nose and puffy eyes, seemed to say: "You are all preventing me from achieving the very important thing I was destined by fate to accomplish, the thing I know how to do better than all of you, and to which I've already devoted most of my conscious life." In the mudroom he ran into the stationmaster's wife and Vasyatka, who immediately took his two traveling cases.

"The seventh house down thataways," explained the station-master, running ahead and opening the door to the porch. "Vasyatka, show the doctor gentleman the way."

Platon Ilich went outside, squinting. The day was frosty and overcast; a faint breeze had been blowing for the last three hours and a fine snow was still falling.

"He won't ask fer too much," the stationmaster mumbled, shivering in the wind. "He ain't much interested in profits. Just as long as he can drive."

Vasyatka put the traveling bags on the porch bench, disappeared back inside, and soon returned in a short fur coat, felt boots, and a hat; he grabbed the traveling bags and stomped the snow that had been swept off the porch.

"Let's go, doctor, sir."

The doctor followed, puffing on his cigarette. They walked along an empty, snow-covered village street. A good deal of snow had accumulated: it reached halfway up the doctor's fur-lined knee-high boots.

"It's coming down hard," thought Platon Ilich, hurrying to finish his cigarette, which was burning quickly in the wind. "What the devil made me take a shortcut through this blasted station? It's a godforsaken place, there are never any horses here in winter. I swore I wouldn't, but, no! I had to go this way, *Dummkopf.* If I'd taken the high road, I'd have changed horses in Zaprudny and driven on, and so what if it's seven versts farther, I'd be in Dolgoye by now. And the station there is well kept, and the road is wide. *Dummkopf!* Now you're out somewhere on a wild goose chase!

Vasyatka energetically tramped through the snow ahead, swinging the identical travel bags like a woman carrying buckets on a yoke. Though the station was called the village of Dolbeshino, it was really just a settlement with ten farmyards scattered a fair distance apart. By the time they'd hiked down the powdery main road and reached the bread man's house, Platon Ilich had begun to sweat a bit in his long coat. Snowdrifts had blown up against the old, sunken loghouse, and it looked like no one lived there. The only signs of human habitation were wisps of white smoke that the wind tore from the chimney.

The travelers passed through a front garden that was fenced off after a fashion, and stepped up onto the sagging, cracked porch, which was almost entirely buried in snow. Vasyatka gave the door a push with his shoulder and it turned out to be unlocked. They stepped into a dark entryway. Vasyatka bumped into something and said:

"Goodness . . . Ouch!" In the darkness, Platon Ilich could

just make out two large barrels, a wheelbarrow, and a pile of junk. For some reason the bread man's mudroom smelled like an apiary: beehives, caked pollen, and wax. The lovely summer aroma was totally at odds with the February blizzard. Vasyatka made his way with difficulty to the burlap-insulated door, opened it, and, grabbing one of the traveling cases under his arm, stepped over the high threshold:

"Hello in there!"

The doctor followed him in, ducking to miss the lintel overhead.

The *izba* was slightly warmer, lighter, and less cluttered than the mudroom: logs burned in a large Russian ceramic stove, a wood salt cellar stood by itself on the table, a round loaf of bread lay under a towel, a lone icon occupied a dark corner, and a pendulum clock hung on the wall like an orphan, stopped at half past six. The only pieces of furniture the doctor noticed were a chest and an iron bed frame.

"Uncle Kozma!" Vasyatka called out, carefully setting the traveling cases on the floor.

No one replied.

"Maybe he's out in the courtyard?" Vasyatka turned his wide freckled face with its ridiculous, peeling red nose toward the doctor.

"What is it?" came a voice from the top of the stove, and a head with tangled red hair, a shaggy beard, and sleepy slits for eyes appeared.

"Hello, Uncle Kozma!" Vasyatka cried out joyfully. "There's a doctor here's in a hurry to get to Dolgoye, but there ain't no horses at the station."

"So?" He scratched his head.

"Well, you could take him there on the sledmobile."

Platon Ilich walked over to the stove:

"There's an epidemic in Dolgoye, and I must be there today, without fail. Without fail!"

"Epidemic?" The bread man rubbed his eyes with big, calloused fingers that had dirty nails. "I heard about it. They was talkin' about it at the post office in Khoprov just yesterday."

"There are sick people waiting for me there. I'm bringing the vaccine."

The head on the stove disappeared, then the stairs creaked and squeaked. Kozma descended, in a fit of coughing, and came out from behind the stove. He was a short and stunted, skinny, narrow-shouldered man about thirty years old, with crooked legs and the kind of oversized hands tailors often have. His nose was sharp. His face, puffy with sleep, was kind and tried to smile. He stood barefoot in his underclothes in front of the doctor, scratching his tousled red hair.

"A vax-seen?" he said respectfully and cautiously, as though he was afraid to drop the word on his worn, cracked floorboards.

"A vaccine," the doctor repeated, and took off his fox-fur hat, which had made him feel overheated right away.

"But there's a blizzard, doctor, sir." Crouper glanced at the dimmed window.

"I know there's a blizzard! And there are sick people waiting for me!" the doctor raised his voice.

Scratching his head, Crouper went to look out the window, which was insulated with hemp chinking stuffed in around the sides.

"I didn't even fetch the bread today." He flicked a patch of window where the hoarfrost had melted from the stove's heat, and looked out. "After all, man don't live by bread alone, ain't that right?"

"How much do you want?" The doctor was losing his patience.

Crouper looked back at him as though he expected to be beaten; he walked silently over to the right of the stove where there were buckets on the bench and shelves with earthenware pots and kettles, picked up a copper ladle, scooped some water out of the bucket, and began to drink so fast his Adam's apple bobbed up and down.

"Five rubles!" the doctor proposed, in such a threatening tone of voice that Crouper flinched.

He began to laugh, wiping his mouth with his shirtsleeve:

"Now what would I be needing . . ."

He put the ladle down, looked around, and hiccupped.

"But, I . . . I just fired up the stove . . ."

"People are dying out there!" the doctor shrieked.

Avoiding the doctor's gaze, Crouper scratched his chest and squinted at the window. The doctor stared at the bread man with such an expression on his tense, large-nosed face, it was hard to tell whether he was ready either to beat him or to burst into tears.

Crouper sighed and scratched his neck:

"Hey, youngster, you just . . ."

"Wha?" Vasyatka opened his mouth, not understanding.

"Sit tight. When it catches—close the flue."

"I'll do that, Uncle Kozma." Vasyatka took off his sheepskin coat, tossed it on the bench, and sat down next to it.

"Your sledmobile . . . what power is it?" the doctor asked in relief.

"Fifty horses."

"Good! We'll be in Dolgoye in about an hour and a half. And you'll drive back with five rubles."

"Come on now, yur 'onor . . ." Crouper smiled, waved his claw-like hand, and slapped himself on his thin haunches. "Alrighty, let's go harness up."

He disappeared behind the stove and soon came out in a thick homemade gray wool sweater and padded pants held up almost to his chest by an army belt; he clutched a pair of gray felt boots under his arm. He sat down on the bench next to Vasyatka, tossed the felt boots on the floor, and began wrapping his footcloths.

The doctor went outside to smoke. Nothing had changed: gray sky, snow, wind. The farm seemed to have died—there wasn't a human voice or dog's bark to be heard.

Platon Ilich stood on the porch and inhaled the refreshing cigarette smoke. He was already thinking about tomorrow: "I'll do the vaccinations at night and in the morning we'll go to the cemetery and take a look at the graves. We have to hope that the weather hasn't interfered with the quarantine; if someone made it through the lea pastures—you'll never find him. In Mirino there were two cordons and even that didn't help—they broke through, and started biting the population . . . I wonder if Zilberstein is there already. I hope he's there! It's easier to vaccinate when you've got four hands. He and I could get through the whole village in one night . . . But no, leaving from Usokh, he won't get there before me . . . It's forty versts, and in this weather . . . Just my luck . . . A storm like this . . ."

Meanwhile, Crouper had put on his boots, thrown on a small black coat and tied it with a sash, tucked a pair of long heavy mittens under the sash, pulled on a hat, picked up a loaf of bread from the table, cut off the heel, and stuck it under his coat; he cut off another piece and took a bite. Still chewing, he winked at Vasyatka, who was sitting on the bench:

"A gulp of tea to warm the bones now, eh? But ain't no time: just looky what a fuss he's making. Epi-demic! Where'd he come in from?"

"Repishnaya, I think." Vasyatka rubbed his eyes with a fist. "With the post horses. The mail driver, he went straight to bed."

"Why shouldn't they sleep, 'em fellers . . ." Crouper took a farewell glance at the stove, cuffed Vasyatka on the head, and went out into the backyard chewing his piece of rye bread.

The bread man's yard was just as plain and old as the *izba*: a lopsided stall abutted it, stores of firewood were piled in disarray, and in the distance was a hay shed with a collapsed roof that had been hastily covered with poles and straw; close by a dark threshing barn looked like it hadn't seen a threshing for at least four years. In contrast, a small stable resembling a bathhouse was new: it had a shingled roof, well-chinked walls, and two insulated windows. Next to it, under a snow-covered lean-to, stood the sledmobile. Crouper plowed through the snow in a fast, bow-legged gait, reached the stable, stuck his hand under his shirt, pulled out a key on a string, and opened the hanging lock.

From behind the door came an intermittent, shrill sound, like the trill of a large cricket. Then three more chimed in, then more, more, and more, until suddenly it seemed an entire swarm of crickets was chirping away noisily. Then came a grunt. The chirping in the stable grew even louder.

"Now, you lot, I'm here, I'm comin' . . ." Crouper unlocked the door, threw it wide open, and entered the stable.

He was met by pleasant, familiar smells. Leaving the door ajar so there would be more light, he walked through the smithy and tack room straight to the horses' stalls. A joyous chirping filled the stable. In contrast to Crouper's miserable hut and yard, his stable was exemplary: spanking new, clean, and tidy, a clear indication of the owner's true passion. The stable was divided in half: the smithy and tack room began right at the door. There was a workbench with a small forge, also a tiny oven the size of a samovar, with a bellows fashioned from a beekeeper's fumigator, and instruments neatly arrayed on the workbench: knives, little hammers, tiny pincers, a gimlet, saws, and a jar of horse ointment with a brush inside. In the middle of the workbench was a ceramic cup filled with tiny kopeck-sized horseshoes. Next to it was another cup that held tiny nails for the shoes. Little wooden yokes were strung in rows on the nearby wall, like dried mushrooms. A large kerosene lantern hung over the forge.

Beyond the forge and tack was the feed in a large woven basket filled with finely cut clover. Then came a partition, and behind it—the horse stalls. Smiling, Crouper leaned over the partition, and the modulating whinnies of fifty small horses filled the air. They occupied various stalls: some in pairs, some five together, some in threesomes. Each stall had two wood troughs— one for water, the other for feed. In the feed trough lay the white remains of the oatmeal Crouper had fed the horses at five that morning.

"Now, the lot of ye—we gonna go for a drive?" Crouper asked his horses, and they neighed even louder.

The younger ones reared and bucked; the shaft horses and the steppe horses snorted, shook their manes, and nodded. Crouper lowered his large, rough hand, still holding the piece of bread in the other, and began petting the horses. His fingers caressed their backs, stroked their manes, and they neighed, tossing their heads and stretching their necks. They playfully nipped his hand with their tiny teeth and pressed their warm nostrils against his fingers. Each horse was no bigger than a partridge. He knew every single one of them and could tell you what its story was, where it was from, and how he got it, how it worked, who its parents were, and describe its likes and dislikes—its personality. The backbone of Crouper's herd, over half of it, consisted of broad-chested bay mares with short, dark red tails. Then came the chestnuts and dark-maned sorrels, eight more bays, four grays, two dapple grays, and two roans—one black roan and one red.

There were only stallions and geldings. *Little mares* were worth their weight in gold, and only horse breeders could afford them.

"Righty, a nice bit of bread," said Crouper as he crumbled the bread and threw it into the troughs.

The horses leaned over. When he'd handed out all the bread crumbs and the horses had finished eating, Crouper clapped his hands and commanded loudly:

"Ha-a-a-rness!"

With a jerk he lifted the gate that opened all the stalls at once.

The horses walked along the cleanly swept wooden chute and mingled in a herd, greeting one another, nipping, whinnying, and bucking. The chute led to a partition wall, behind which the sled stood. Crouper gazed at the herd; his face brightened and he looked younger. His horses always made him happy, even when he was tired, drunk, or feeling downtrodden. He slid back the partition, letting the horses into the harness of the sledmobile. The herd moved briskly despite the cold billowing from the sled's frozen interior.

"There ye go, there ye go," Crouper encouraged the horses. "Ain't so bad, you c'n stand the cold . . ."

He waited for the last horse to enter, then slid the partition shut, quickly went outside, locked the stable, and hid the key under his coat. Hurrying around the stable with a bowlegged gait, he raised the hood of the sled. The well-trained horses had moved into place and were waiting to be harnessed. There were five rows of ten horses under the hood. Crouper quickly pushed the horses' heads through the collars and strapped them in. They went peacefully; only the two bays in the third row began to bicker and disturb the peace, as usual.

"Ye just wait, I'll give ye a taste of the whip!" Crouper threatened them.

Harnessed up, the first row of ten well-fed shaft horses, all bays, pawed the frozen ribs of the drive belt. The chestnuts in the third row lowered their long-maned heads for their master, so he could place them in their collars, while the bays held themselves with the dignity of the highest order of the equine race, their ears perked forward. The grays kept on munching indifferently, the sorrels snorted and tossed their heads, and the dappled grays pranced impatiently. The energetic red roan neighed, baring his young teeth.

"There ye goes." Crouper slid the wooden bolt of the hood across, locking all the horses in place; he took the tar pot, smeared the bearings of the drive belt, put on his mittens, grabbed a small whip, and went to fetch the doctor.

The doctor was standing on the stoop, smoking the last of his second *papirosa*.

"We c'n go, yur 'onor, sir," Crouper informed him.

"Thank God . . . ," said the doctor, flicking his cigarette butt with an annoyed gesture. "Let's be off, then."

Crouper took one of the doctor's travel bags and they walked back through the mudroom and into the courtyard, to the sled.

Crouper unfolded the bearskin rug, the doctor seated himself, and while Crouper strapped his bags to the coach box in back, the doctor examined the horses. He seldom had occasion to see little horses and even less to travel by them, and though tired from the wait, he regarded them with interest as they stood in five rows under the hood, their little hooves striking the ribbed strip of the frozen drive belt.

"Small creatures, and yet they come to our aid in difficult, insurmountable circumstances . . . ," he thought. "How would I have continued on without these tiny beasts? It's strange . . . all hope now lies with them. No one else will take me to this Dolgoye . . ."

He recalled the two ordinary horses that had brought him to this accursed Dolbeshino three and a half hours ago; they were utterly exhausted by the blizzard and were now lodged in the station stables, probably munching on something.

"The larger the animal, the more vulnerable it is to our vast expanses. And humans are the most vulnerable of all . . ."

The doctor stretched out his gloved hand, splayed his fingers, and touched the rumps of the two dark bays in the last row. The little horses glanced at him indifferently.

Crouper approached, sat down next to the doctor, fastened the rug, took up the reins, and flicked his whip:

"And off we go! Heigh-yup!"

He made a clicking sound with his tongue. The horses strained, and their hooves scraped against the drive belt; it responded with a screech and began to move under them.

"Heigh-yup! Ha!" cried Crouper as he whirled the whip over their heads.

The muscles of their small hindquarters rippled, the horses' yokes creaked, the hooves scraped against the drive belt, which began to turn, turn, turn. The sled set off, and the snow squeaked under the runners.

Crouper stuck the whip back in its case and took hold of the reins. The sled was moving out of the yard. There weren't any gates left, all that remained of them were two crooked posts. The sled moved between them, Crouper maneuvered it onto the high road and, smacking his lips, winked at the doctor:

"Off we go!"

The doctor raised his coat's baby-beaver collar in satisfaction, and slid his hands under the rug. They soon left the high road: Crouper turned at the fork; to the left the road led to distant Zaprudny; to the right, Dolgoye. The sled turned right. The road was covered with snow, but here and there occasional mile-posts and bare, wind-tossed bushes could be seen. The snow kept falling: flakes the size of oats fell on the horses' backs.

"Why aren't they covered?" asked the doctor.

"Let 'em breathe a bit, there'll be time to cover up," Crouper replied.

The doctor noticed that the driver was almost always smiling.

"A good-hearted fellow . . . ," he thought, and asked:

"So, then, is it profitable to keep little horses?"

"Well, how's to put it." Crouper's smile widened, exposing his crooked teeth. "So far it's enough for bread and kvass."

"You deliver bread?"

"That's right."

"Live alone?"

"Alone."

"Why's that?"

"My fly got stuck."

"Hmm . . . impotence," the doctor realized.

"But were you married before?"

"I was." Crouper smiled. "For two years. Afterward, when I buttoned up, I come to see that I ain't got the knack for a woman's body. Who's gonna wanna live with me?"

"She left you?" asked the doctor, straightening his pince-nez.

"Left. And thank God."

They rode on silently for a verst or so. The horses didn't run very fast on the drive belt, but they weren't slow either; you could tell that they were well tended to and well fed.

"Doesn't it get lonely by yourself out there on the farmstead?" asked the doctor.

"No time for bein' lonely. In the summer I haul hay."

"And in the winter?"

"In the winter I haul . . . you!" Crouper laughed.

Platon Ilich chuckled.

Crouper somehow made him feel good, and calm; his usual sense of irritation left him and he stopped rushing himself and others. It was clear that Crouper would get him there no matter what happened, that he'd make it in time to save people from that terrible illness.

There was something birdlike in the driver's face, the doctor thought, something that seemed a bit mocking, but at the same time was helpless, kind, and good-natured. This sharp-nosed, smiling face with its sparse reddish beard and swollen squinting eyes, swimming in a large old fur hat with earflaps, swayed next to him in time with the movement of the sled, perfectly happy with everything: the sled, the cold, his well-kept, smooth-gaited little horses, and this fox-fur-hatted doctor in a pince-nez who had appeared out of nowhere with his important travel bags—and even with the endless white plain that stretched far ahead until it drowned in a blur of swirling snow.

"Do you hire out for wagon trains?" the doctor asked.

"Naw, why shud I . . . The job pays enough. I used to work in Soloukhi for some folks, then I figured out that another's bread goes down like lead. So I just stick to haulin' my own bread. And thank God . . ."

"Why do they call you 'Crouper'?"

"Ah . . ." The driver grinned. "From when I was young and I worked at the border. We was cuttin' a road through the forest. Lived in barracks. I caught the croup, was up all the night long. Everbody's sleepin' and here I am coughin' up a storm, they cain't get a wink all night. They got good and mad at me and piled on the work: 'You's coughin' all night, don't give us no peace, so you go chop all the wood, light the fire, draw the water!' They gave it to me good for that croup, they sure did. That's what they'd say: 'Crouper, do this! Crouper, do that!' I was the young'un in the crew. It just stuck: 'Crouper! Hey, Crouper!'"

"Your name is Kozma?"

"Kozma."

"Well, then, Kozma—you don't cough at night anymore?"

"Nope! The Lord looked out for me. Got a bit of ague in the back when the weather's bad. But I'm healthy."

"And you deliver bread?"

"That I do."

"Isn't it a bit unnerving to make the deliveries all alone?"

"Naw. By your lonesome is just fine, yur 'onor. The old-timers had a saying: Drive by your lonesome, you got an angel on each shoulder; drive in a pair, one angel to share; but drive in a troika, and the devil'll grab the reins."

"Wisely put!" The doctor laughed.

"And that's the livin' truth, yur 'onor. When the wagon train's comin' back—the whole string of 'em'll turn off somewheres to drink up their pay."

"And you don't drink?"

"I drink. But I knows my limit."

"Now that's surprising!" The doctor chuckled as he wriggled around under the rug, trying to take out his cigarette case.

"What's the surprise in it?"

"Bachelors usually drink."

"If'n someone brings smoked fish by—I'll drink. But I don't keep none at home. What for? No time fer drink, yur 'onor—I got fifty horses to watch over, after all."

"I see, I see." The doctor tried to light his cigarette, but the match blew out.

The second blew out as well. The wind had risen noticeably, and the snow fell in large flakes on the horses' backs, wedged itself into the corners of the hood, tickled the doctor's face, and made a slight shushing sound on his pince-nez.

He lit up, and peered ahead:

"How many versts to Dolgoye?"

"'Bout seventeen."

The doctor remembered that the stationmaster had said it was fifteen.

"Can we make it in a couple of hours in this weather?" Platon Ilich asked.

"Who knows? Hard to say." Crouper grinned, pulling his hat down to his eyes.

"The road is smooth."

"Right hereabouts it's a good'un." Crouper nodded.

The road ran along a field lined with bushes, so it could be seen even without the rare mileposts that stuck up out of the snow. The field soon gave way to a sparse forest, and the mileposts ended, but sleigh tracks merged into the road, marking the path ahead of them, and encouraging the doctor: someone had just recently traveled along this road.

The sled moved along the sleigh tracks; Crouper held the reins loosely, and the doctor smoked.

Soon the forest grew taller and thicker, the road began to descend, and the sled entered a birch grove. Crouper yanked the reins:

"Whoooaa!"

The horses stopped.

Crouper got down and fussed about under the hood.

"What happened?" asked the doctor.

"Gonna cover the horses," the driver explained, unfurling a burlap tarp.

"Good idea," the doctor agreed, squinting in the windstorm. "It's snowing."

"It's snowing." Crouper covered the hood with the canvas tarp, fastening it at the corners. He sat back down and smacked his lips: "Heigh-yup!"

The horses set off again.

"It's calmer in the forest—there's just one road, you can see it, no way to get lost . . . ," thought the doctor. He brushed the snow from his collar.

"How long ago did you decide to use the little horses?" the doctor asked Crouper.

"'Bout four years ago."

"Why was that?"

"My little brother as lived in Khoprov, Grisha, he died. He left twenty-four horses. And his wife, stands to reason, didn't wanna take care of 'em. She says: 'I'm gonna sell 'em.' Then God's angel up and made me ask her: 'How much?' 'Three apiece.' And I had sixty rubles right then. I says: 'I'll buy 'em for sixty.' So we made a deal. I put 'em in a basket and brought 'em back with me to Dolbeshino. Then I got lucky: our bread man, Porfiry, he went off to live in town with his son. I bought his sled fer a good price, and traded a radio fer more horses. And took his place delivering bread. Thirty rubles. That's what we got to live on."

"Why didn't you buy an ordinary horse?"

"Oooorrrrdinaar-y!" Crouper puckered his lips and stretched them forward, which made him look just like a jackdaw in profile. "Cain't cut enough hay fer an ordinary one. I'm on my lonesome, yur 'onor, like a heron standin' in a swamp, wher'm I gonna sow that hay! Even fer a cow you cain't never cut enough hay. I don't even keep a cow no more, got rid of it. But fer the little ones—nothin' to it: I plant a row of clover, cut it down, dry it—and it'll last 'em the whole winter. Grind some oats fer 'em, give 'em a little water—quick as a wink and that's the end of it."

"But these days people keep big horses, too," the doctor pointed out. "In Repishnaya we have a family that keeps a big horse."

"But that's a family, yur 'onor!" said Crouper, shaking his head so hard that his hat slipped down even further over his eyes.

Adjusting his hat, he asked the doctor:

"What kinda horse is it?"

"Twice the size of regular ones."

"Twice? That ain't much. I seen bigger'uns at the station. You see the new stable there?"

"No."

"In the fall they builded a ginormous one. I heard tell on the radio how at the Nizhny market there was a cart horse tall as a four-story building."

"Yes, there are horses that size." The doctor nodded seriously. "They're used for extra-heavy work."

"You seen 'em?"

"I've seen them from a distance, in Tver. A draught horse that size was pulling a coal train."

"Whaddye know!" exclaimed Crouper with a click of the tongue. "How much oats do a horse like that eat in a day?"

"Well," said the doctor, squinting ahead and wrinkling his nose, "I think that . . ."

Suddenly the sled jerked and twisted, and a crack was heard; the doctor nearly flew headlong into the snow. Underneath the tarp the horses snorted.

"What . . ." Crouper only had time to exhale, as his hat fell off and he tumbled chest-first onto the steering rod.

The doctor's pince-nez sailed off his nose and got tangled in the lace attached to it. He caught it and put it back on. The sled stood at the side of the road, listing to the right.

"Darn you . . ." Crouper slid down, rubbing his chest. He walked around the sled, squatted, and looked underneath it.

"What's the problem?" asked the doctor without getting up.

"We banged into somethin' . . ." Crouper moved to the right side of the road and immediately plunged into deep snow; he turned over, grunting, and squeezed under the sled.

The doctor waited in the listing sled. Finally Crouper's head appeared:

"Just a sec . . ."

He threw back the tarpaulin, which the falling snow had already covered, and pulled back on the reins, without returning to his seat:

"C'mon now, c'mon . . ."

The horses, snorting and huffing, began to prance backward. But the sled simply sputtered in place.

"Why don't I get off . . ." The doctor unfastened the bearskin and stepped down.

"C'mon now, c'mon!" Crouper pushed against the sled, helping the horses backstep.

The sled jerked backward, once, twice, and moved off of the unfortunate spot. It came to a halt crosswise on the road. Crouper ran around to the front and squatted. The doctor came over in his long, hooded coat. The tip of the right runner was split.

"There ye go, damnation . . . Ugh!" Crouper spat on the snow.

"It cracked?" asked the doctor, leaning over to get a closer look.

"It splitted," Crouper said in an anguished voice, making a squelching sound.

"What did we hit?" asked the doctor, looking in front of the sled.

There was only loose snow, and new flakes falling on it. Crouper began to rake the snow away with his boot, and suddenly kicked something hard, which slid out. The driver and passenger leaned over, trying to see what it was, but couldn't make out anything. The doctor wiped his pince-nez, put it on again, and suddenly saw it:

"*Mein Gott* . . ." He reached down cautiously.

His hand touched something smooth, hard, and transparent. Crouper got down on all fours to look. A transparent pyramid about the size of Crouper's hat could just barely be discerned in the snow. The passenger and driver felt it. It was made of a dense, clear, glasslike material. The storm swirled snowflakes around the perfectly even facets of the pyramid. The doctor poked it— the pyramid easily slid to the side. He took it in his hands and stood. The pyramid was extraordinarily light; indeed, one could almost say that it weighed nothing at all. The doctor turned it in his hands:

"What the devil . . ."

Crouper looked it over, wiping the snow off his eyebrows:

"What's that?"

"A pyramid," said the doctor, wrinkling his nose. "Hard as steel."

"That's what hit us?" asked Crouper.

"Apparently." The doctor turned the pyramid around. "What the hell is it doing here?"

"Maybe it fell off a wagon?"

"But what's it for?"

"Oh now, yur 'onor . . ." Crouper brushed the snow away in annoyance. "Nowadays there's so many things that ye cain't figure out what they's for . . ."

He grasped the broken tip of the runner and moved it carefully:

"Looks like it didn't break all the ways."

With a sigh of returning irritation, the doctor tossed the pyramid aside. It disappeared in the snow.

"Yur 'onor, we gotta tie that runner with somethin'. And turn right back 'round the way we come." Crouper wiped his nose with his mitten.

"Back? What do you mean, back?"

"We only gone 'bout four versts. But down there in the hollow the snow's bound to be deeper, and we'll get stuck with a runner what's tied. And that'll be the end of the story."

"Wait, what do you mean, go back?" said the doctor. "People are dying out there, orderlies are waiting, there's an epi-dem-ic! We can't go back!"

"We've got our own . . . epi-demic." Crouper burst out laughing. "Just take a look-see how that runner splitted."

The doctor squatted and examined the cracked runner.

"Cain't go twelve versts with that. Lookit how the blizzard's comin' on." Crouper glanced around.

The blizzard had indeed grown more intense, and the wind whirled the snow about faster.

"We'll make it through the forest, and then we'll get stuck in the hollow at the bottom—and that'll be it. We'll be in a real pickle."

"What if we wrap it with something?" asked the doctor, examining the runner and brushing off the falling snow.

"What with? A shirt? We c'n tie it up but it ain't gonna last long. It'll come aparts. I don't wanna go lookin' for trouble, yur 'onor."

"Wait, wait, just a minute . . ." The doctor tried to think. "Damned pyramid . . . Listen, what if . . . I've got elastic bandages. They're strong. We'll bandage it up good and tight and be off."

"Bandage?" Crouper was perplexed. "A bandage's weaker than a shirt, it'll pull off right straightaway."

"Elastic bandages are strong," the doctor declared gravely as he stood up.

He said this with such conviction that Crouper fell silent and shuddered. He suddenly had the shivers.

The doctor strode over to his travel bags, unfastened one of them, opened it, quickly found a package of stretch bandages, and grabbed it. He noticed a vial and various ampoules in his travel bag, and exclaimed joyfully:

"I've got an idea! An idea!" He took one of the vials and hurried over to the runner.

Crouper kneeled next to him and scraped the snow aside with his mittens. He felt another pyramid.

"How 'bout that, another one," he said, showing it to the doctor.

"To hell with it!" The doctor kicked the pyramid and it flew off.

He slapped Crouper on the back:

"Kozma, you and I will fix everything! If you had instant glue, would you glue the runner together?"

"Sure I would."

"Well, then, we're going to spread this ointment on here, it's very thick and sticky, and then we'll wrap the runner with a bandage. In this cold the ointment will harden and pull your runner together. You'll be able to drive to Dolgoye and home five times with a runner like this."

Crouper looked mistrustfully at the vial. The label read: VISHNEVSKY OINTMENT + PROTOGEN 17W.

The doctor uncorked the top and handed it to Crouper:

"It hasn't had time to harden yet . . . Dip your finger in and spread it on the runner."

Crouper pulled off his mittens and took the vial carefully with his big hands, but immediately gave it back to the doctor:

"Wait . . . Then we gotta put somefin under . . ."

He swiftly pulled an axe out from beneath the seat, walked into the forest, chose a young birch tree, and began to hack away.

The doctor set the vial down on the sled, stuck the bandage roll in his pocket, took out his cigarette case, and lit up.

"It's coming down hard . . . ," he thought, squinting at the whirling snowflakes. "Thank God it's not all that cold, it's not cold at all, really . . ."

Hearing the sound of the axe, the horses began to snort under the tarp; the lively red roan whinnied delicately. A few other horses answered him.

Crouper had felled the birch, chopped off a log, and sharpened it against the birch stump before the doctor had finished his *papirosa*.

"There ye go . . ."

Having completed his task, he returned to the sled, breathing hard, and deftly thrust the birch wedge under the middle of the right runner. The tip lifted slightly. Crouper brushed away the snow under it:

"Now we'll rub it on."

The doctor gave him the vial and proceeded to unwrap the bandage packaging. Crouper lay down on his side next to the runner and rubbed the ointment along the crack in the wood.

"Just figures," he muttered. "I run straight into tree stumps a coupla times, and nothin' happens, but now, one bump and it might as well been a cleaver . . . Bloody damnation."

"Don't worry, we'll bandage it up and we'll make it there," the doctor consoled Crouper while he watched him work.

The moment Crouper had finished, the doctor pushed him aside impatiently: "Come on, out of the way . . ."

Crouper rolled away from the runner. The doctor, grunting, sat down on the snow and then heaved himself over on his side, adjusted his position, and began to skillfully wrap the bandage.

"Now then, Kozma, you press the crack together and hold it!" he managed to gasp.

Crouper grabbed the tip and pressed the sides together.

"Excellent . . . excellent . . ." the doctor muttered as he continued to wrap the runner.

"Gotta tie the ends up top, else it'll get cut off on the bottom," Crouper advised.

"Don't teach the teacher . . . ," the doctor wheezed.

He wrapped the runner tight and even, tied the ends up top, and expertly tucked them under the bandage.

"That's the ticket!" Crouper smiled.

"What did you expect?" roared the doctor victoriously. He sat up, panting, and banged his fist on the side of the sled. "Let's go!"

Inside, the horses neighed and snorted.

Crouper knocked the wedge out from under the runner, tossed the axe on the footboard, took off his hat, wiped his sweaty brow, and looked at the snow-dusted sled as though he were seeing it for the first time:

"Still, maybe we oughta go back, eh, yur 'onor, sir?"

"N-n-n-no!" The doctor stood up and brushed the snow off his coat, shaking his head in an insulted, threatening gesture. "Don't even dare think about it. The lives of honest workers are in danger! This is an affair of state, man. You and I don't have the right to turn back. It wouldn't be Russian. And it wouldn't be Christian."

"'Course not." Crouper plopped his hat on. "Christ be with us. Cain't do without 'im."

"That's right, brother. Let's go!" The doctor clapped him on the shoulder.

Crouper laughed, sighed, and gestured with his hand: "At yur service!"

Crouper threw back the snow-covered bear rug and sat down. Having fastened his own traveling bag in back, the doctor sat down next to Crouper, and wrapped himself in the rug with an expression of satisfaction and the feeling of an important job successfully accomplished.

"How're ye doin' in there?" Crouper looked under the tarpaulin.

In reply came friendly neighs from the horses, who had been standing in place all this time.

"Thank the Lord. Heigh-yup!"

The horses' hooves scrabbled against the drive belt, then the sled trembled and moved. Crouper straightened it out, and steered it in the right direction. Glancing at the road, both riders noticed immediately that during the time they'd been working on the runner, snow had covered all trace of the sleighs that had traveled the path earlier; the road that lay ahead of them was white and untouched.

"Whoa, just look at all the snow—a herd of elephants couldn't pack it down." Crouper clicked his tongue and tugged on the reins. "Quick, let's go now, faster."

The horses, who'd been bored under their tarp, didn't need any encouragement: they ran energetically on the frozen drive belt, their little shoed hooves tapping noisily. The sled started briskly across the fresh snow.

"If'n we cross the ravine, up 'bove past it, the road is good all the ways to the mill!" Crouper shouted, frowning in the snowy wind.

"We'll make it!" the doctor encouraged him, hiding his face under his collar and fur cap, leaving only his nose, which had turned slightly blue, out in the open.

The wind blew large snowflakes about and swirled them into snowdrifts. The forest was sparse on either side, with clear indications of felled timber.

The doctor saw an old dry oak that had apparently been split by lightning many years before, and for some reason he remembered the time. He took out his pocket watch and checked it: "Past five already. How we've dawdled . . . Well, no matter . . . There's no traveling fast in this kind of snow, but if we can keep at this crawl, we should make it in a couple of hours. How did we manage to run into that strange pyramid? What is it for? Must be some sort of table decoration—it's clearly not a tool or machine. The transport must have been overloaded, carrying lots like it; one fell out and ended up under the sled . . ."

He remembered the crystal rhinoceros in Nadine's house, the rhinoceros that stood on the shelf with her sheet music, the music she picked up with her small fingers, placed on the piano, and played, turning the pages with a brisk, abrupt movement, the kind of movement that instantly conveyed her impulsive nature, unreliable as ice in March. That sparkling rhinoceros with its sharp, crystal horn and dainty tail, curled like a pig's, always looked at Platon Ilich with a hint of mockery, as though teasing him: remember, you're not the only one who's walking on thin ice.

"Nadine is already in Berlin," he thought. "There's never any snow there in winter. It's probably rainy and dank. In the Wannsee, the lake never even freezes over, ducks and swans swim there all winter . . . Their house is nice, with that stone knight, the centuries-old linden trees and sycamores . . . How stupidly we parted. I didn't even promise to write to her . . . When I get back I'll definitely write to her, immediately, enough playing the insulted and injured—I'm not insulted and I'm not injured . . . And she's marvelous, she's wonderful, even when she's nasty . . ."

"We should have taken that pyramid with us," he said suddenly, and glanced at the driver.

Crouper, who didn't hear him, drove along with his usual birdlike expression. He was happy that the sled was riding smoothly, as though it had never broken down, happy that his beloved horses were feeling lively, and that the blizzard wasn't bothering them.

"How d'ye like that, it don't even pull to one side," Crouper thought, moving the steering rod with his right hand and holding the reins with his left. "Means the doctor bound the runner right. He's got the knack and knows his business. Serious he is, that one. What a big nose. Just drive him to Dolgoye, ain't nothin' else will do. Doctors, they's seen terrible sights, and knows a lot. Back last year that feller went under the thresher at Komagon's, and in the city they sewed his leg on, and it grew back, runs faster'n it used to . . . And me, when my teeth acted up, that doctor in Novoselets, he give me a shot and opened up my jawbone . . . It didn't hurt one bit, he took out three teeth, and half a cup of blood . . ."

The road sloped down, the forest grew even sparser, and ahead of them in the snowy mantle of the blizzard the vague contours of a large ravine arose.

"Right about here's where we gotta hurry, yur 'onor," said Crouper, "else mine won't make it to the top in this kinda snow. After all, they ain't three-story cart horses . . ."

"Let's hurry, then!" the doctor answered cheerfully, turning around.

They jumped off the sled and immediately sank knee-deep in snow. The road was entirely blanketed. Crouper wedged the steering rod in a straight position, grabbed the back of the sled where traces of old flaking painted decorations could be seen, and began to run, pushing from behind. But the sled had barely passed the bottom of the ravine and started up the other side when it began to lose speed and then stopped completely. Crouper threw back the tarp and asked the horses: "What's the matter?"

He flapped his mitten over their backs:

"C'mon, then, the lot of ye! C'mon, give it a tug!"

He let loose a loud whistle.

The horses leaned into the drive belt and Crouper pushed from the back. The doctor helped as well.

"Fas-ter! Fas-ter!" Crouper screeched.

The sled moved, crawling upward with great difficulty. But it soon stopped again. Crouper braced it from behind so it wouldn't slide down into the ravine. The horses snorted. The doctor was about to fling himself at it again, but Crouper stopped him. Breathing heavily, he spat into the snow:

"Wait a bit, yur 'onor, we'll get our strength back . . ."

The doctor was also out of breath.

"Not long now." Crouper smiled, tilting his hat back. "Don't worry. We'll make it up in a bit."

They stood, catching their breath.

Large, soft snowflakes fell thickly, but the wind seemed to have died down and was no longer throwing snow in their faces.

"I didn't think it was so steep here . . . ," said the doctor, leaning against the sled and looking around while he turned his broad, snow-covered hat.

"Right here's a stream," said Crouper, breathing heavily. "In the summer ye gotta ford it. The water's good. When I comes this way I always get down fer a drink."

"I hope we don't slide backward."

"Naw, we won't."

After a bit, Crouper whistled and cried out to the horses:

"C'mon now or I'll let you have it! Give it a tug! Tuug! Tug!"

The horses scraped at the drive belt. The passenger and the driver pushed the sled. It crawled slowly up the hill.

"C'mon! C'mon!" Crouper shouted and whistled.

But twenty paces on they came to a halt once again.

"You . . . damn . . ." The doctor slumped limply against the back of the sled.

"Just a minute, yur 'onor, just a minute . . . ," Crouper muttered in a stifled voice, as though defending himself. "You'll see, after this we'll go sliding down real easy-like, all the way to the ponds . . ."

"Why on earth did they put the road here . . . where it's so steep . . . Idiots . . . ," the doctor puffed indignantly, shaking his hat.

"Where's else to put it, yur 'onor?"

"Go around it."

"But how could ye go around it here?"

The tired doctor waved his hand, indicating that he wasn't about to argue. After catching their breath, they once again crawled upward to the sound of Crouper's cries and whistles. They had to pause and rest another four times. When they finally emerged from the ravine, both the humans and the horses were exhausted.

"Thank the . . ." was all Crouper managed to gasp; he spat back at the accursed ravine and went to check the horses under the hood.

Steam rose from the little horses. They were in a lather, though it could hardly be seen: while they were making their way out of the ravine, twilight had descended. The exhausted doctor took off his hat, wiped off the sweat dripping from his head and brow, then took out a handkerchief and blew his nose like a horn. His thin white scarf had slipped out from under his coat and was dangling from his neck. The doctor scooped up a handful of snow and greedily stuffed it in his mouth. Crouper covered the horses, then kicked off his felt boots and shook out the snow that had gotten into them. Stumbling, the doctor climbed up onto the seat, leaned back, and sat with his face lifted to the falling snow.

"Well now, we made it." Crouper put his boots back on, sat down next to the doctor, and gave him a tired smile. "Let's go?"

"Let's go!" the doctor almost screamed, fumbling for his cigarette case and matches in his deep, silk coat pockets, which were so delightful to the touch. The sensation of the familiar, soft, cozy silk calmed him and reassured him that the worst was now behind them, that the anxiety of the dangerous ravine was a thing of the past.

Platon Ilich lit a cigarette with the special pleasure of a person resting after heavy work. His narrow, overwrought face exuded heat.

"Want a cigarette?" he asked Crouper.

"Ever so grateful yur 'onor, but we don't smoke." The driver tugged on the reins and the horses pulled weakly.

"Why is that?"

"Never happened to." Crouper smiled a tired, birdlike smile. "I'll drink vodka, but don't take tobacco."

"Good for you!" The doctor smiled, just as tired, and blew smoke out of his full lips.

The horses worked quietly, and the sled drove over a snow-laden road, laying down its own path. The forest ended at the ravine; ahead, through the whirling snow a sloping field with the occasional island of bushes and willow reeds could be discerned.

"They're exhausted, they are, my little horses." Crouper slapped his mitten on the tarp. "Don't worry, it'll go easier now."

The road began a gentle turn to the left, and fortunately a milepost appeared here and there.

"We pass the pond, and then the road's straight through New Forest, cain't hardly get lost," Crouper explained.

"Let's do it, my man," the doctor encouraged him.

"They'll rest a bit, and we'll ride on."

Hauling the sled at an unhurried pace, the horses gradually recovered from the torturous hill. They rode along like this for about two versts. By then it was almost completely dark. The snow fell thick, and the wind was still.

"Over there's the mill pond." Crouper pointed ahead with his whip, and the doctor thought he saw a large, snow-covered haystack in front of them.

They drew closer, and the haystack turned out to be a bridge over a stream. As they crossed it, something scraped at the bottom of the sled. Crouper grabbed the steering rod to straighten the angle, but the sled abruptly swerved to the right; it careened off the bridge, stopping in a snowdrift.

"Ay, damnation," Crouper exclaimed.

"Don't tell me it's the runner again," muttered the doctor.

Crouper jumped down, and his voice sounded:

"All right now, c'mon! C'mon! C'mo-on!"

The horses began backstepping obediently. Crouper threw his weight against the front of the sled and heaved. The sled barely made it out of the snowdrift; Crouper disappeared into the wintry shroud, but returned quickly:

"It's the runner, yur 'onor. Your bandages come off."

Irritated and exhausted, the doctor unfastened the rug, descended, and walked around the sled. He leaned over, barely able to distinguish the cracked tip of the runner.

"Damn it!" he cursed.

"Uh-huh." Crouper snuffled.

"We'll have to bandage it again."

"What fer? We'll go a coupla versts and it'll come off again."

"We must go on! We absolutely must!" The doctor shook his hat.

"Stubborn, he is . . ." Crouper looked at him, scratched his head under his hat, and gazed into the distance:

"Here's what I'll tell ye, yur 'onor. The miller lives near here. We'll hafta go there. It'll be easier to fix the runner."

"A miller? Where?" asked the doctor, turning all about, seeing nothing.

"Over yonder, where the window's lit up," said Crouper, flapping his mitten.

The doctor peered into the snowy darkness and was indeed able to make out a faint light.

"I wouldn't go to his place for ten rubles of money. But ain't no choice. Don't want to catch our death out here."

"What's wrong with him?" the doctor asked distractedly.

"Cusses. But his wife's a good woman."

"Well, then, let's go right this instant."

"Only let's walk, 'cause the horses're too tuckered to pull."

"Let's go!" The doctor headed directly for the light and sank into snow up to his knees.

"Thataway's the road!" Crouper pointed.

Swearing and stumbling in his full-length coat, the doctor reached the utterly invisible road. Crouper strained to direct the sled, but he urged the horses on, walking next to them and holding the steering rod.

The road snaked along the banks of a frozen river, and the sled crept forward at an agonizing pace. Crouper grew tired and out of breath steering it. The doctor walked behind, giving the back of the seat an occasional push. Snow fell, thicker and thicker. At times the snowfall was so dense the doctor thought they were making circles around the bank of a lake. Now and then, the light ahead vanished completely, and then a twinkle would appear.

"We just had to run over that pyramid," thought the doctor, grasping the back of the sled. "We would have been in Dolgoye a long time ago. This Kozma is right—there are so many pointless things in the world . . . Someone manufactures them, transports them to cities and villages, convinces people to buy them, and makes money on bad taste. And people do buy them, they're thrilled, they don't even notice the uselessness, the stupidity of the thing . . . It was just that sort of idiotic object that caused us so much harm today . . ."

Constantly correcting the sled, which kept bearing right, off the road, Crouper thought about the hateful miller, about how he'd already vowed to himself two times that he'd never go near there again. Now here he was once more, and he'd have to have dealings with him.

"Musta made a weak vow," he thought. "I vowed on Commemoration I'd never set foot . . . and now here I am a runnin' to him for help. If'n the vow was strong enough, nothin' woulda happened, the angels woulda carried me over that mill on wings. And now—rush, knock, beg . . . Maybe I shouldn't make no vows? Like Grandpa said: Don't do no harm, and don't make promises . . ."

Finally, ahead of them two willows arose, half buried in snowdrifts, and beyond them was the miller's house with its two lit windows, perched right on the riverbank, almost hanging over the water. Through the snowstorm the frozen waterwheel looked to the doctor like a round staircase leading into the river from the house. The image was so convincing that he didn't question it but assumed that the staircase was a necessary part of the household, used for something important having to do, most likely, with fishing.

The sled inched up to the miller's house.

A dog began to bark behind the gates. Crouper got down, walked over to the house, and knocked on the lit window of a gatehouse. After a while, the gatehouse door opened a bit and someone, invisible in the dark, spoke out:

"What is it?"

"Hey there," said Crouper, approaching him.

"Oh, you." The person who'd opened the little gate recognized Crouper.

Crouper recognized him as well, although this was only the worker's first year with the miller.

"I, um, I'm taking the doctor here to Dolgoye, and our runner broke, and it's not too convenient to fix it out in the wind."

"Ah . . . Just a minute . . ."

The little gate closed.

Several long minutes passed, then behind the gate there was some movement, the bolts clanked, and the gates started to open with a squeak.

"Enter the yard!" the very same worker shouted in a commanding voice.

Crouper smacked his lips loudly, directing the sled through the gateposts. It slid into the courtyard and the doctor walked in after it. The worker immediately shut and locked the gates. Though it was dark and snowy, the doctor could nonetheless discern a fairly spacious courtyard with a number of buildings.

"Mr. Doctor, welcome," came a woman's voice from the porch.

The doctor headed toward the voice.

"Watch your step, don't trip," the voice warned.

Platon Ilich could barely make out the door, and he tripped on the step; his hand grabbed the woman.

"Don't trip," she repeated, supporting him.

The woman exuded a sour country warmth. She held a candle,

which immediately went out. The woman was the worker's wife. She led the doctor through the mudroom entrance and opened the door.

The doctor entered a spacious *izba*, richly appointed by village standards. Two large kerosene lanterns illuminated the space: there were two ovens, one Russian, one Dutch; two tables, kitchen and dining; benches, trunks, shelves for dishes, a bed in the corner, a radio under a cozy; a portrait of the sovereign in an illuminated, iridescent frame, and portraits of his daughters Anna and Ksenia in the same type of frame. A double-barreled pistol and a Kalashnikov were hung on moose antlers, a tapestry depicting deer at a watering hole was attached to the wall, and a vodka still rested on a wooden stand.

The miller's wife, Taisia Markovna, sat at the table; she was a large, portly woman about thirty years old. The table was set with a small round samovar and a two-liter jar of homemade vodka.

"Welcome, please come in," the miller's wife said, rising and adjusting the colorful Pavloposad shawl that had slipped from her round shoulders. "Goodness gracious, you're all covered in snow!"

The doctor was indeed completely covered with snow. He looked like a snowman children make at Shrovetide—except for his bluish nose, which protruded from beneath his big, snow-covered fur hat.

"Avdotia, don't just stand there, give him a hand," the miller's wife ordered.

Avdotia started brushing the snow off the doctor and helped him to take off his coat.

"Why on earth were you traveling at night, and in such a

snowstorm?" The miller's wife came from behind the table, her skirt rustling.

"When we left it was light," the doctor answered, handing over his heavy, wet clothes, and remaining in his dark-blue three-piece suit and white scarf. "We broke down along the road."

"How horrible." The miller's wife smiled, approaching the doctor, holding the end of her scarf in her plump white hands.

"Taisia Markovna," she bowed to the doctor.

"Dr. Garin." Platon Ilich nodded at her, rubbing his hands.

As soon as he entered the *izba* he realized that he was freezing, exhausted, and hungry.

"Have tea with us, it will warm you up."

"Gladly." The doctor took off his pince-nez and squinted at the samovar as he began to wipe the lenses gingerly with his scarf.

"Where have you come from?" the miller's wife asked.

Her voice was deep and pleasant; she spoke in a slight singsong and her accent wasn't local.

"I left Repishnaya this morning. It turned out there weren't any horses in Dolbeshino, so I had to hire a local driver with his own dray."

"Who?"

"Kozma."

"Crouper?" squeaked a little voice at the table.

The doctor put on his pince-nez and looked: next to the samovar, a little man sat on the table with his legs dangling over the edge. He wasn't any bigger than the shiny new little samovar. His clothes were small, but entirely in keeping with the clothes of a prosperous miller: he wore a red knit sweater, mousy gray wool trousers, and stylish red boots, which he swung back and forth. The man held a tiny hand-rolled cigarette, which he had just finished gluing with his little tongue. His face was unattractive, pale, and he had no eyebrows. The sparse fair-colored hair sticking up from his head turned into a sparse light beard on his cheeks.

The doctor had often had occasion to see and treat little people, and thus he showed no surprise. He retrieved his cigarette case, opened it, and took out a *papirosa*. Screwing it into the corner of his fleshy lips with an accustomed gesture, he answered the little fellow:

"Yes, that's him."

"Well, some driver you found yourself!" The little man laughed nastily, putting his homemade cigarette in his unpleasant, large mouth and taking out a lighter the size of a three-kopeck coin from his pocket. "The devil knows where that guy'll take you."

He struck his lighter, a stream of blue gas flared, and the little man stretched the lighter up toward the doctor.

"Crouper? Where is he?" The miller's wife turned to look at the maid, her calm brown eyes slightly shiny from vodka.

"In the barnyard," the maid answered. "Should I call him?"

"Of course, tell him to come in, he can warm up."

The doctor leaned down toward the little man, who stood politely, the lighter thrust upward forcefully, as though he were holding a torch. His hand shook, and it was clear that he was drunk. The doctor lit his *papirosa*, stood up straight, inhaled, and then exhaled a wide stream of smoke over the table. The little man bowed slightly to the doctor:

"Semyon, Markov's son. Miller."

"Dr. Garin. You and your wife have the same patronymic?"

"Yes!" the little man chuckled, and swayed, steadying himself against the samovar, then snatching his hand back immediately.

"Markovna and Markich. Just turned out that fucking way . . ."

"Don't swear," said the miller's wife, coming over. "Sit down, doctor, have your tea. And there's no sin in having a bit of vodka in this weather."

"No, no sin," agreed the doctor, who really wanted a drink.

"Of course! Vodka after tea keeps the soul frost-free!" the miller squeaked. He staggered over to the jar, embraced it, and gave it a ringing slap.

He was the same height as the bottle.

The doctor sat down, and Avdotia set a plate, a shot glass, and a three-pronged fork in front of him. The miller's wife picked up the bottle, pushing aside the miller, who sat down abruptly on the table, bumping his back against a hunk of wheat bread. She filled the doctor's glass: "Here's to your health, doctor."

"What about me?" whined the miller, dragging on his little cigarette.

"You've had enough already. Sit there and smoke." The miller didn't argue with his wife; he just sat, leaning against the bread, puffing away.

The doctor lifted the shot glass and downed it quickly and quietly, still holding a *papirosa* in his left hand; he caught some sour cabbage on his fork and had a bite. The miller's wife placed a piece of homemade ham on his plate, and potatoes fried in lard.

"Anything else, Markovna?" Avdotia asked.

"That's it. Go about your business. And tell Crouper to come in here."

Avdotia left.

After taking several deep drags on his *papirosa*, the doctor quickly stubbed it out in a small granite ashtray full of tiny cigarette butts, and began to devour the food.

"Crouuuu-per!" the miller drawled, skewing his froglike lips, which were already ugly enough. "She went and found the dear guest. Crouper! Just a bum, that scum!"

"We're always pleased to have guests," the miller's wife said calmly, pouring herself some liquor; she smiled at the doctor and ignored her husband. "To your health, doctor."

Platon Ilich's mouth was full, so he nodded silently.

"Pour *me* some!" whined the miller.

Taisia Markovna set down her glass, sighed, picked up the bottle, and splashed some vodka into the steel thimble that stood on a tiny plastic table. The doctor hadn't immediately noticed the standard plastic table made for little people standing between the dish with the ham and the cup with pickles. The thimble gleamed on the little table, which held glasses and plates with the same food as the big table for regular people, slivers sliced from the larger portions: a snippet of ham, a dab of lard, a piece of pickle, bread crumbs, a marinated mushroom, and some cabbage.

Taking one last drag on his cigarette, and blowing the smoke out with an unpleasant, serpentine hiss, the miller tossed the butt down, stood up, and with a grand gesture stomped it out with his boot. The doctor noticed that the soles of his red boots were copper. The miller picked up the thimble and stretched unsteadily toward the doctor.

"Here's to you, Mr. Doctor! To our dear guest! And against any sort of scummy riffraff."

The doctor chewed, watching the miller silently. The miller's wife again filled his glass. The doctor clinked glasses with each of them. They all drank: the doctor downed his glass just as quickly and quietly; Taisia Markovna drank slowly, with a sigh, her large bosom heaving; and the miller drank with a tormented backward toss of his head.

"Whew!" The miller's wife exhaled, pursing her small lips like a straw. She sighed, adjusted the shawl on her shoulders, crossed her plump hands on her high bosom, and examined the doctor.

"Whoa!" the miller grunted. He banged his empty thimble on the little table, grabbed his crumbs, held them to his nose, and sniffed loudly.

"How did you come to break down?" the miller's wife asked. "Or did you hit a tree stump?"

"That's about what happened," the doctor agreed, and stuffed a piece of ham in his mouth, as he had no desire to tell the bizarre story of the pyramid.

"What do you expect from Crouper? He's an asshole!" the miller squawked.

"Oh, you think everybody's an asshole. Let me talk with the man. Where did it happen?"

"About three versts from here."

"Must have been in the ravine." The miller picked up a little knife and stumbled over to the pickles, speared one, and cut off a piece like a wedge of watermelon. He stuffed it in his mouth and crunched noisily.

"No, it was before the ravine."

"Before?" Taisia Markovna caught her breath. "But the road's wide, even though it goes through forest."

"Huh, that half-wit drove off the road, hmmm, and straight into a birch tree . . ." The miller nodded, still chewing on his pickle.

"We hit something hard. Bad luck. But my driver's good."

"He's good," the miller's wife agreed. "Markich here just doesn't like him. He doesn't like anyone."

"I like . . . Don't tell lies . . . ," said the miller with his mouth full.

Suddenly he spit out the chewed-up pickle with a snort and stamped his foot:

"I like you, stupid! Don't argue with me."

"Who's arguing?" His wife laughed, looking at the doctor. "And where are you going, from Repishnaya?"

"To Dolgoye."

"To Dolgoye?!" She stopped smiling and her face looked shocked.

"To Dolgoye?!" the miller screeched and stood stock-still.

"To Dolgoye," the doctor repeated.

The miller and his wife looked at each other.

"They've got the black plague, we saw it on the radio," said Taisia Markovna, raising her black eyebrows in surprise.

"I saw it on the radio this morning!" The miller nodded his head. "They've got the black plague!"

"Yes. The black sickness." The doctor nodded as he finished chewing and leaned against the back of the chair.

His large nose had turned red and sweaty from the vodka and food. He took out a handkerchief and blew his nose loudly.

"They've . . . The . . . There's troops on the outskirts. Where do you think you're going?" The miller staggered back and stumbled.

"I'm bringing the vaccine."

"Vaccine? To inoculate them?" the miller's wife asked.

"That's right. To vaccinate the ones who are left."

"The ones that d-d-didn't get bit yet?" Stepping back once more, the miller reclined on the pickle.

It was clear that the last thimbleful had knocked him off his feet.

"Yes. The ones that haven't been bitten yet."

The doctor retrieved a cigarette from his case and lit up with the satisfied sigh of a man who has assuaged his hunger.

"Aren't you afraid to go there?" asked the miller's wife, her bosom heaving.

"That's the nature of my job. And what's to be afraid of? The troops are there."

"But they . . . mmm . . . Those . . . They're . . . quick ones," she said, her plump hand spinning her empty glass in worry.

"They! The-e-y! Oh, they're quick ones, they are! They are so qui-i-i-ck!" shouted the miller, holding on to a bump on the pickle, and shaking his head, as though offended.

"They can tunnel underground." She licked her lips.

"Tunnel! That's right! They tunnel under!"

"And they can come out anywhere at all."

"And they c-c-can . . . They c-can! Those dirty . . ."

"They can, of course," agreed the doctor. "Even in winter they have no trouble digging their way through frozen earth."

"Lord Almighty," said the miller's wife, crossing herself. "Are you armed?"

"Of course." The doctor puffed on his *papirosa*.

He liked the miller's wife. There was something maternal, kind, and cozily caring about her that brought back memories of childhood, when his mother was still alive. The miller's wife wasn't beautiful, but her femininity was winning. Talking to her was a pleasure.

"That drunkard got lucky," the doctor thought, looking at her plump hands and her smooth, pudgy fingers, with their tiny nails, which were spinning the drinking glass.

The door opened and Crouper entered.

"Oho! It's Iva-an Susanin!" The miller burst out laughing,

holding on to the pickle. "What were you doing, running into a birch tree? A birdbrain, that's what you are."

"Really, it's true—a birdbrain," the doctor agreed silently. He looked at Crouper.

"Greetings!" Crouper took off his hat, bowed, crossed himself in front of the icon, and began to remove his snowy clothes.

"Who said you could do that?" the miller objected. "Asshole!"

"Stop cursing, Senya." The miller's wife slapped her heavy hand on the table.

"You're an enemy of the s-s-state. Got it? A s-s-sa-saboteur!" The miller, staggering around the hors d'oeuvres, crossed the table toward Crouper. "They should sh-sh-ut you up for it!"

He tripped and planted himself on the lard.

"Just sit there!" grinned the miller's wife. "Come in, Kozma. Have a seat."

Crouper smoothed his red, sweaty hair and sat down at the table.

"All those scummy bums should be locked up . . . You're a fucking asshole!" the miller screeched, staring nastily at Crouper.

"Now, now . . ." Losing patience, the miller's wife scooped up her husband and put him on her bosom, pressing him tightly. "Sit!"

Holding on to her husband with one hand, she poured some vodka into a tea glass for Crouper:

"Drink," she said. "It will warm you up."

"Thank you, Taisia Markovna."

Crouper sat down at the table, picked up a glass with his clawlike hand, leaned over it, opened his magpie mouth, and began slowly sucking in the moonshine, straightening up as he drank.

When he finished, he exhaled, frowned, took a piece of bread, sniffed it, and put it on the table.

"Have a bite, Kozma, don't be shy."

"Go on, stuff your face!" the miller chortled.

And then the miller began to sing in a tremulous voice:

> There was an old woman from Tula,
> Said, "I'm off to the States to make moolah."
> "You stupid old cunt," her old man did swear,
> "They ain't got no trains that go there."

"Now you stop that!" The wife poked the miller.

He laughed tipsily.

Crouper stuck a piece of lard in his mouth, bit off some bread, and chewed rapidly. He'd just swallowed when the doctor asked him:

"What about the sled?"

"The steering rod? Pulled it out, nailed it back."

"Does it work?"

"Yup."

"Then let's get going."

"You're going to travel? To Dolgoye?" The miller's wife smiled grimly.

"They're waiting for me."

"Ah, go on . . . Let that rag pile go. The doctor can stay!" The miller shook his fist at Crouper.

"Hold on now!" Taisia Markovna pressed her husband to her bosom. "You can't go off into the storm at night. You'll lose the road straightaway."

"S-s-straight! Away!" The miller shook his head.

"I absolutely must get to Dolgoye today," the doctor asserted stubbornly.

The miller's wife sighed deeply, rocking her husband like a baby:

"You'll get across the grove, and the old village, but that's where the fields start and there's no mileposts either. You'll get stuck in the field. You have to spend the night."

"Can't anyone show us the way? Your worker, for instance?"

"What?" The miller's wife grinned. "You think he has cat eyes? He can't see at night. And he's not from around here."

"He's just the g-guy you want . . ." The miller dug his boots into his wife's chest, climbed up to her neck, and stared at Crouper. "And you there, you just . . . take that!"

The miller gave Crouper the finger. Crouper was eating cabbage slaw and paid no attention to him.

"Stay till morning." With her free hand the miller's wife set a glass under the samovar tap and turned the spigot. Boiling water poured into the glass.

"They're expecting me today." The doctor stubbed out his cigarette.

"Even if you don't get lost, you still won't make it till morning time. Leave now and you'll not go far."

"Maybe we oughta stay, doctor, sir?" Crouper asked timidly.

"You jess get th'ell outta! Ya lost a horse at the market! You loser loafer!!" the miller shouted, kicking his feet against his wife's bosom.

"Stay now, don't be silly." The miller's wife poured strong brew from a Chinese teapot. "The storm will die down, and you'll fly along."

"And if it doesn't?" The doctor looked at Crouper as though the weather depended on him.

"If'n it don't, it's a sight calmer in the light," Crouper answered. Something stuck in his throat and he had a coughing fit.

"He lost the horse to passs-churs, lost traaa-ck-o-vvvit!" The miller refused to quiet down. "They oughta lock ye up fer horse-thieving!"

"Stay." The miller's wife set the glass of tea down in front of the doctor and began to pour some for Crouper.

"And the horses c'n rest a piece."

"No snoozin', not a wink . . . They'll rest in peace, not rest a piece, thass whachur horses'll do!" cackled the miller.

The miller's wife laughed, her chest rose, and her husband rocked on it as though on a wave.

"Maybe we really should stay?" thought the doctor.

He looked around for a clock on the well-chinked wall, but didn't see one; he was about to take his pocket watch out but suddenly saw small, glowing numbers hovering in the air over a metal circle lying on the sewing machine: 19:42.

"We could try to get there by midnight . . . But if we get lost, as she pointed out . . . ," the doctor thought.

He took a sip of tea.

"We could stay and leave at first light. If the blizzard has stopped, we'll get there in an hour and a half. If I give them vaccine-2 eight hours later, nothing terrible will happen. That's acceptable. I'll write an explanatory note . . ."

"Nothing terrible will happen if you get there tomorrow," said the miller's wife, as though she'd read his mind. "Have some more vodka."

Deep in thought, the doctor bit his lower lip and glanced at the numbers glowing in the air.

"So we're staying?" Crouper asked, no longer chewing.

"Very well." Platon Ilich sighed with disappointment. "We're staying."

"Thank God!" Crouper nodded.

"Yes, thank God," the miller's wife almost sang, as she filled the glasses.

"What about me? What about me?" The miller tottered and swayed on her chest.

She dripped a few drops from the bottle into the thimble and handed it to the miller.

"May you be healthy!" She raised her glass.

The doctor, Crouper, and the miller all drank.

Taking a bite of ham, the doctor now looked at the room not just as a stopping place but as the night's lodging: "Where will she put us? In another *izba*? We had to end up here for the night. Damn this blizzard . . ."

Crouper took a deep breath and relaxed. He warmed up right away and was glad that he wouldn't have to go out into the dark now, glad not to get lost looking for the road, torturing himself and his horses; glad that his horses would spend the night in the warmth of the miller's stable, that he would give them some oats—he always had a bag of oats stored under the seat—and that he himself would sleep here, most likely on top of the stove, in the warmth, and that the nasty miller couldn't touch him; glad that they'd leave early the next morning, and that when he'd delivered the doctor to Dolgoye, he'd get five rubles and drive back home.

"Oh well, perhaps it's for the best," said the doctor, reassuring himself.

"It's for the best." The miller's wife smiled at him. "I'll put you upstairs, and Kozma—on the stove. It's quiet and warm upstairs."

"Ow, what the . . . Got a leg cramp . . . ," the miller squeaked, grabbing his right leg, his drunken face grimacing.

"Time for bed." The miller's wife picked him up to take him off her chest, but at that moment the miller dropped the thimble. It rolled down his wife's large body and fell under the table.

"Now look what you've done, Semyon Markich, gone and lost your cup." Lovingly, as though he were a child, the miller's wife placed him in front of her on the edge of the table.

"Huh? Whass, how's . . . the . . . what?" muttered the thoroughly drunk miller.

"That's what," she replied. Standing, she lifted her husband with two hands, carried him over to the bed, set him down on it, and drew the curtains.

"Lie down, time to go night-night." She rustled the pillows and blanket, tucking her husband in.

"Wake me up early tomorrow," the doctor told Crouper.

"The crack of dawn, first light," the driver replied, nodding his reddish magpie-shaped head.

It was obvious that the vodka, warmth, and food had made Crouper tipsy, and that he was ready to sleep.

"Let 'em all . . . all o' them . . . 'em all . . ." The miller's drunken squeak could be heard behind the curtain.

"Sorta like a cricket . . . chirp chirp," Crouper thought, smiling his birdlike smile.

"Taa-iiii-sssia . . . Taiss . . . Let's cuddle and have a roll in the hay," the miller peeped.

"We will, we will. Sleep tight."

Taisia Markovna emerged from behind the curtains, walked over to the guests, squatted, and looked under the table.

"It's somewhere . . ."

"A handsome woman," the doctor thought all of a sudden.

Squatting and looking under the table with her marvelous, cloudy eyes, she awoke his desire. She wasn't pretty, that was particularly noticeable now, when the doctor saw her face from above. Her brow was a bit low; her chin heavy and tilted downward; all in all her face adhered to the typically crude peasant model. But her carriage, her white skin, her buxom bosom, rising and falling, aroused the doctor.

"There it is." She reached under the table and bent over.

Her hair was woven into a black braid, and the braid wound round her head.

"A delicious woman the miller has . . . ," the doctor thought, and suddenly, ashamed of his thoughts, he gave a tired sigh and laughed.

The miller's wife stood up; smiling, she showed him her little finger with the thimble on it.

"There you go!"

She sat down at the table:

"He likes to drink out of my thimble, though we have glasses."

And indeed—on the miller's table, amid the little plates, there was a little glass.

"I c'd go to sleep now," Crouper said with a hint of complaint in his voice as he turned his tea glass upside down.

"Go on, love." The miller's wife took the thimble off her finger and placed it upside down on the overturned glass. "There's a pillow and a blanket atop the stove."

"Mighty grateful, Tais' Markovna." Crouper bowed to her and climbed up on top of the tile stove.

The doctor and the miller's wife remained alone at the table.

"So then, you do your doctoring in Repishnaya?" she inquired.

"Yes, in Repishnaya." The doctor took a gulp of tea.

"Is it hard?"

"Sometimes. When people are sick frequently—it can be difficult."

"And when is the sickness greater? In winter?"

"Epidemics happen in the summer, too."

"Epidemics," she repeated, shaking her head. "We had one about two years back."

"Dysentery?"

"That's it. Something got into the river. The kids swimming took sick."

The doctor nodded. There was clearly something about the woman sitting opposite him that excited him. He looked her over furtively, a bit at a time. She sat calmly, a little smile on her face, and regarded the doctor as if he were a distant relation who'd stopped by when he saw the lights on. She didn't seem particularly interested in the doctor and spoke with him the same way she did with Crouper and Avdotia.

"Is it boring for you here in winter?" asked Platon Ilich.

"A bit."

"Summer's probably fun, no?"

"Oh, summer . . ." She raised her hands. "Summer is bustling, something every which way you turn."

"People bring their grain to the mill?"

"Of course they do!"

"Are the other mills far from here?"

"Twelve versts, in Dergachi."

"So there's plenty of work."

"There's plenty of work," she repeated.

They sat in silence. The doctor drank tea, the miller's wife played with the end of her kerchief.

"Should we watch the radio?" she suggested.

"Why not," said the doctor, smiling.

He really didn't want to say goodnight to this woman and go upstairs to sleep. The miller's wife rose and took a knitted cover off the receiver, picked up the black remote control, returned to the table, turned down the lamp wick, sat back down in her chair, and pressed the red button on the remote. The radio clicked and a round hologram with a thick number "1" in the right corner appeared above them. Channel 1 had the news: a story about the reconstruction of the automobile plant in Zhiguli; another about a new single-occupancy sledmobile with a potato-fueled engine. The miller's wife switched to Channel 2. A regular church service was on. The miller's wife crossed herself and glanced at the doctor. He stared indifferently at the middle-aged priest in raiment and the young deacons. She turned to the last channel, Channel 3, the entertainment channel. They were showing a concert, as always. First, two beauties in sparkling traditional headgear sang a duet about a golden grove. Then a jolly, broad-faced fellow, winking and clucking, sang about the cunning intrigues of his indefatigable, atomic mother-in-law, causing the miller's wife to laugh a few times, and a weary smirk to appear on the doctor's face. Then the young men and girls began a long dance on the deck of the *Yermak*, a steamship sailing down the Yenisei River.

The doctor dozed.

The miller's wife turned the set off.

"I can see you're tired," she said, rearranging the scarf, which had slipped off her shoulder.

"I'm . . . not . . . the least . . . bit . . . tired," the doctor mumbled, shaking off his stupor.

"You're tired, tired." She rose. "Your eyes are shutting. It's time for me to get some sleep, too."

The doctor stood up. Despite his bleary drowsiness, he didn't want to part with the miller's wife.

"I'll go out for a smoke." He took off his pince-nez, wiped the bridge of his nose, and blinked his swollen eyes.

"Go ahead. I'll get everything ready."

The miller's wife left, her skirts rustling.

"She'll be upstairs," the doctor thought, and his heart pounded. He heard two snores—one slight, Crouper, from the stove; the other, from behind the curtain, sounded like the chirr of grasshoppers.

"Her husband's asleep . . . A drunken swamp rat. No, a watery drunk! A mill pond drunk!"

The doctor burst out laughing, took out a *papirosa*, lit it, and left the room. Passing through the cold, dark mudroom entrance, he bumped into something and had trouble finding the door to the courtyard; eventually, he pulled back the bolt and stepped outside.

It was windy, but the snow had stopped and the sky was clear; the moon shone through tufts of dark clouds. "It's settled down," said the doctor, puffing on his cigarette.

"We could even leave now." He walked to the middle of the courtyard, mounds of snow crunching underfoot.

But his heart was pounding, sending jolts of hot longing through him.

"No, I'm not going anywhere . . ."

"Tomorrow!" he said decisively. Clenching his *papirosa* between his teeth, he walked over to the woodpile and relieved himself.

A dog barked in the cowshed.

The doctor quickly finished smoking and tossed the *papirosa* in the snow.

"Does she usually sleep with her husband on the bed behind the curtain? Where else would she sleep? So big and white, and next to her he's like some child's doll."

He stood, taking in the invigorating, frosty air, and looking up at the stars that twinkled between the moving clouds. The moon peeked out and illuminated the courtyard: the storehouse, a shed, snow-capped haystacks—everything gleamed in the fresh, new-fallen snow, in myriad snowflakes. The snow-dusted courtyard and the frigid calm exuded by the wood, which, once upon a time, people had shaped and nailed together into these buildings—all this only intensified Platon Ilich's desire. The contours of the immobile woodshed, filled with hundreds of frozen birch logs and kindling, all doomed to a brilliant death in the stove, seemed to tell him: in that house there is something warm, alive, trembling, on which the whole human world rests and upon which all its woodsheds, villages, sleds, cities, epidemics, airplanes, and trains depend. And this warmth, this femininity, awaits your desire, your touch.

Shivers ran down the doctor's spine; he shuddered, shrugged his shoulders, exhaled, and went back into the house. Passing through the entryway, he felt for the door to the kitchen, opened it, and was immediately met with another dusky darkness. The lamp wasn't burning, but there was a candle on the table.

"I made the bed for you upstairs," called the voice of the miller's wife. "Goodnight."

Judging by the voice, she was already lying on the bed behind the curtain. Crouper and the miller were still snoring. Adding to the racket was the chirp of a real cricket, responding amusingly to the miller's cheeps.

The doctor heaved a sigh, not knowing what to do. He wanted to ask the miller's wife something, find an excuse to stay, but then he quickly realized how ridiculous it would seem, and, all in all, how stupid and vulgar his thoughts were. He was suddenly ashamed.

"Idiot!" he cursed himself. "Good night."

"Don't kill yourself on the stairs. Take the light," came her voice, barely audible, from the darkness of the main room.

The doctor took the candle from the table and went silently upstairs. The staircase led to the attic directly from the entry-way; the steps were narrow and creaked under the doctor's boots.

"Idiot. A regular idiot!"

Upstairs there were two rooms: in the first were woven baskets, chests, boxes, strings of onion, garlic, and dried pears. The garden aroma was soothing. The doctor passed that room; the door to the other one was ajar. He found himself in a small room with a dark window, a bed, a little table, a chair, and a small dresser. The bedclothes were turned back.

The doctor set the candle on the table, closed the door, and began to undress.

"Beddy-bye, the calf's asleep." Noticing a clay cow on the windowsill, he remembered the children's rhyme.

"What a strange family . . . Though perhaps it isn't strange, but quite normal for the times. And they live well, prosperously . . . For how long? How old is she, I wonder . . . thirty?"

He recalled her calm hands, the ring on her pinky finger, and the look of her dark-brown eyes.

"*Guten Abend, schöne Müllerin* . . . ," he said aloud, recalling Nadine's beloved Schubert. He took off his shirt.

"One should never abandon one's principles. As in chess, one should not stoop lower than the floor and make forced moves. Coercion is not the way to live—the palliatives of work are more than enough. Life offers choice: one should always choose what comes naturally, what will not cause you to regret your own lack of willpower later in life. Only epidemics leave you no choice."

Remaining in his underclothes, he removed his pince-nez, placed it on the table, blew out the candle, and climbed into the cold bed. Upstairs, as always, it was chilly.

"A good night's sleep." The doctor pulled the blanket right up to his nose. "And leave bright and early tomorrow. As early as possible."

There was a soft knock at the door.

"Yes?" The doctor raised his head.

The door opened and a burning candle appeared. The doctor picked up the pince-nez from the table and put it to his eyes. The miller's wife entered the room inaudibly, barefoot; she wore a long white nightgown and her colorful shawl around her shoulders. She held the burning candle in one hand and a cup in the other.

"Forgive me, I forgot to leave you water. Our ham's so salty, you'll be wanting a drink in the night."

She leaned over, and her loose hair fell from her shoulders to her breasts as she set the cup on the table. Her eyes met the doctor's, her face as calm as ever. She blew out the candle and straightened up. And remained.

The doctor tossed his pince-nez on the table, threw back the blanket in one movement, stood up, and embraced her warm, soft, large frame.

"There we go . . . ," she said softly, putting her hands on his shoulders.

He drew her toward the bed.

"I'll close the door . . . ," she whispered in his ear, and his heart pounded like a hammer.

But he didn't want to let her go. He pressed against her body and his lips found her neck. The woman smelled of sweat, vodka, and lavender oil. In one movement he tore off her nightgown and grabbed her by the butt.

Her bottom was big and plushy and cool.

"Oh . . . ," she murmured.

The doctor threw her back on the bed; trembling, he began tearing off his underclothes. But neither the clothes nor his hands would obey. "Damn . . ." He pulled hard and a button flew off and rolled across the floor.

Having managed to get one leg free of his hateful underwear, he fell on her and spread her smooth, plump legs roughly with his own. Her legs opened obediently and bent at the knees. In an instant, trembling and panting, he entered the substantial body, which gave itself to him. She moaned and embraced him.

He grabbed her by the round, sloping shoulders he had admired at the table, made a few spasmodic thrusts, and couldn't contain himself: his seed flooded into her.

"Sweetheart." She pressed her head to his with a calming movement.

But he could not calm down. He did not want to calm down. He squeezed her, and began to push, as though racing to catch up with the desired body slipping away from him. Her legs opened wider, letting him in, and her warm hand slid down his back and grabbed his rear. The doctor's movements were brusque. He seized the woman in his arms and dug his fingers into her. His backside trembled and squeezed tight in time with his movement. As if to calm it, the woman's hand began to press down gently. The doctor panted noisily into her neck, and his head shuddered.

"My sweetheart."

She pushed down on his buttocks, sensing the fury of the contracting muscles.

"My sweet . . ."

Her hand soothed him, as if to say with its every move: there's no hurry, I'm not going anywhere, I'm yours tonight.

He understood the language of that hand; the convulsions left his body and he began to move more slowly, rhythmically. With her left hand the woman lifted his hot head and brought her lips to his parched, open mouth. But he didn't have the strength to respond to her kiss. He took intermittent, greedy breaths.

"My sweet . . . ," she exhaled into his mouth.

The doctor had her; trying to stretch out the pleasure, he obeyed her delicate feminine hand. Her body responded to him, her wide hips squeezed his legs in time with his movement: they opened and squeezed, opened and squeezed. Her ample chest rocked him.

"My sweet," she exhaled into him once again. And her breath seemed to sober him up. He answered her kiss, their tongues meeting in the hot darkness of their bodies.

They kissed.

Her hand stroked and calmed him. Understanding that the man was ready to enjoy her for a long while, the woman gave herself to him utterly. A moan began in her large, heaving breast. And she allowed herself to be helpless. Her breasts and hips trembled.

"Plow me, my sweet . . . plow me," she whispered into his cheek, and gripped him with both arms.

He swam in her body and the wave continued, rolling further and further, till it seemed it would never end.

But the wave suddenly surged; he understood his helplessness, and his body trembled in anticipation. Her hand once again touched his buttocks, but its touch was no longer gentle, it was forceful, commanding. The hand pushed and clutched him, and her fingers dug into him as though each one wore a thimble.

With a roar he spurted into the wave.

The woman moaned and cried out under him. He lay on top of her, exhaustedly breathing into her neck.

"Hot . . . ," she whispered, and stroked his head.

The doctor caught his breath, then turned over and lifted his head.

"Strong . . . ," she said.

He sat upon the edge of the bed and looked at the miller's wife in the darkness. Her body took up the entire bed. The doctor put his hand on her chest. She immediately covered his hand with her palms: "Have a drink of water."

The doctor remembered the cup, picked it up, and drank the water thirstily. The moon peeked out from behind the clouds and poured light in through the window. The doctor was able to locate his pince-nez, so he put it on. The miller's wife lay with her chubby hands behind her head. The doctor stood and fumbled in his trouser pockets for his cigarette case and matches. He lit up, and sat back down on the edge of the bed.

"I didn't think you'd come to me," he said in a hoarse voice.

"But you wanted me to." She smiled.

"I did," he said with a doomed sort of nod.

"And I wanted to also."

They gazed at each other silently. The doctor smoked, and the light of the *papirosa* was reflected in his pince-nez.

"Let me have a smoke, too."

He handed her the *papirosa*. She inhaled, held the smoke for a while, then let it out carefully. The doctor watched. He suddenly realized he had absolutely no desire to talk to her.

"You're a bachelor?" she asked, and returned the cigarette to him.

"You can tell?"

"Yes."

He scratched his chest:

"My wife and I split up three years ago."

"You left her?"

"She left me."

"So that's what happened," she said respectfully.

They sat quietly.

"Any children?"

"No."

"How come?"

"She couldn't conceive."

"Ah, so that's it. I gave birth, but it died."

They sat silently again.

The silence stretched on and on.

The miller's wife sighed and sat up on the bed. She put her hand on the doctor's shoulder: "I'll go now."

The doctor said nothing.

She turned over on the bed and the doctor squeezed to one side. She lowered her plump feet to the floor, stood up, and straightened her nightgown, while the doctor sat with the extinguished cigarette in his mouth.

The miller's wife stepped toward the door. He took her hand: "Wait."

She sat back down.

"Stay a bit longer."

She pulled a lock of hair back from her face. The moon moved behind clouds and the room was plunged into darkness. The doctor caressed her; she touched his cheek:

"Is it hard without a wife?"

"I'm used to it."

"May God help you meet a good woman."

He nodded. She stroked his face. The doctor took her hand in his and kissed the sweaty palm.

"Come see us on the way back," she whispered.

"It won't work out."

"You'll go a different way?"

He nodded. She moved closer, lightly touching him with her breast, and kissed his cheek:

"I'll go now. My husband will be mad."

"He's asleep."

"He gets cold without me. Too cold, and he'll wake up and start whining."

She stood up.

The doctor didn't try to keep her any longer. Her nightgown rustled in the dark, the door squeaked and closed, and the steps of the staircase creaked under her bare feet. The doctor took out another *papirosa*, lit it, rose to his feet, and walked to the window.

"*Guten Abend, schöne Müllerin* . . . ," he said, gazing at the dark sky hanging over the snowy field.

He smoked his cigarette, stubbed it out on the windowsill, got in bed, and fell into a deep, dreamless slumber.

Crouper also slept soundly. He fell asleep as soon as he got up on the warm oven bed, put a log under his head, and covered himself with the patchwork quilt. Falling asleep to the sound of the doctor's strong, nasal voice chatting with the miller's wife, he thought of the toy elephant that his late father had brought six-year-old Kozma from the fair. The elephant could walk, move its trunk, flap its ears, and sing an English song:

Love me tender, love me sweet,
Never let me go.
You have made my life complete,
And I love you so.

After the elephant he thought of the horse the drunken miller
kept harping on. Vavila, the late merchant Riumin's groom, had
entrusted Crouper with the horse. This was at the fair in Pokrovskoye, before Kozma got married, but when he was already known
as "Crouper." Vavila had a year-old colt for sale, and he had been
walking around the fair with him all morning, trying to sell him.
He got greedy, and thought some Chinese people and Gypsies
were trying to cheat him. He asked Kozma to hold on to the colt,
said he was going to "stuff his face and take a dump." He gave
Kozma five kopecks. Kozma found a spot by the willow, near
where the saddler's stalls began. He stood there with the colt
and cracked sunflower seeds. Right about then some movie people from Khliupin put up two receivers and stretched "tableau
vivant" screens between them. They displayed dolphins. It turned
out that the picture wasn't just lifelike, but *touchable*; the dolphins swam from one screen to the other and you could touch
them. First kids and then men and women came up to touch the
dolphins. Crouper tied the colt to the willow and waded through
the crowd. He reached out and touched a dolphin. He liked it.
The dolphin was smooth and cool, and it made friendly, squeaky
noises. And the sea was nice and warm. Pushing his way forward, Crouper entered the water up to his chest and kept on
touching and touching. The dolphins dove down in one monitor
and swam over to the other one. Crouper touched their backs
and stomachs, and grabbed them with his hands, trying to hold
on to them. But they were agile and slipped right out of his

grasp. He felt happy and fell in love with dolphins then and there. When the movie fellows turned the picture off and went around the crowd with a hat out, Crouper threw in his five-kopeck coin without a thought. Then he remembered the colt and went back to the willow: there was no trace of the horse. Vavila chased Crouper through the fair and landed a few good punches. The merchant Riumin sacked Vavila. They never found the colt.

The doctor awoke to the sound of Crouper's voice:

"Yur 'onor, sir, it's time."

"What is it?" the doctor grumbled with his eyes closed.

"The dawn's up."

"Let me sleep."

"You asked me to wake ye."

"Go away."

Crouper left.

Two hours later the miller's wife climbed up to the doctor's room and touched his shoulder:

"It's time for you to go, doctor."

"What?" the doctor murmured with his eyes closed.

"It's already eleven o'clock."

"Eleven?" He opened his eyes and turned over.

"Time for you to get up." She looked at him with a smile.

The doctor fumbled for his pince-nez on the side table, placed it on his wrinkled face, and looked up. The miller's wife hung over him—large, nicely dressed in a fur-lined top with a string of viviparous pearls on her neck, braids circling her head, and a pleased, smiling face.

"What do you mean, eleven?" the doctor asked more calmly, finally remembering everything that had happened during the night.

"Come and have tea." She squeezed his wrist, turned, and disappeared behind the door, her long blue skirt rustling.

"Damn . . ." The doctor stood up and looked at his watch. "It really is eleven."

He looked at the window. Daylight flooded through it.

"The idiot didn't wake me." The doctor remembered Crouper and his magpie-shaped head.

He dressed quickly and went downstairs. The kitchen was bustling: Avdotia was sliding a large kettle into the recently lit Russian oven with a long-handled poker; her husband was making something on the bench in the corner; and at the far table the miller's wife sat majestically alone. The doctor headed for the washbasin that stood in the corner to the right of the oven, splashed his face with cold water, and dried it with a fresh towel that the miller's wife had hung there especially for him. He wiped his pince-nez, looked at himself in the small, round mirror, and touched the stubble on his cheeks:

"Hmm . . ."

"Doctor, come have a cup of tea," the strong voice of the miller's wife sounded from the other side of the room.

Platon Ilich went to her.

"Good morning."

"And a very fine morning to you, too." She smiled.

The doctor crossed himself before the icon and sat down at the table. The same little samovar stood on the table and the same ham lay on a dish.

The miller's wife poured tea into a large cup with a portrait of Peter the Great, and dropped in two sugar cubes without asking.

"Where's my driver?" asked the doctor, looking at her hands.

"On the other side. He's been up for quite a while now."

"Why didn't he wake me?"

"Can't say." She smiled pleasantly. "Some fresh blini?"

The doctor noticed a stack of piping-hot pancakes on the table.

"Gladly."

"With jam, honey, or sour cream?"

"With . . . honey."

He frowned. He felt uncomfortable with the woman now.

"What drama . . . ," he thought as he sipped the tea.

"How's the weather?" He glanced at the windows.

"Better than yesterday," answered the miller's wife, looking him straight in the eye.

"A strong woman . . . ," he thought, and remembering her little husband, he cast his eyes about the room.

The miller was nowhere to be seen.

"He's still sleeping," she said, as though she'd read the doctor's mind. "Got a hangover. Eat up."

She set a plate of blini in front of him and slid the honeypot over. The doctor began eating the delicious, warm blini. Crouper entered the room and stopped at the door. He was dressed for the road and held his hat in hand.

"There's our hero . . . ," the doctor grumbled. He swallowed a piece of pancake and almost shouted:

"Why didn't you wake me?"

Crouper smiled his birdlike smile:

"How's that I didn't wake ye? Went right upstairs come first light."

"And . . . ?"

"I says: Doctor, time to go. And you says: Let me sleep."

The miller's wife laughed and poured tea into her saucer.

"That's impossible!" The doctor banged his fist on the table.

"As the Lord's my witness," Crouper said, waving his hat toward the icon.

"Well then, that means you were having a good sleep." The miller's wife blew on the tea in the saucer.

The doctor met her pleasant eyes and glanced at the other people in the room, as though seeking their support. Avdotia was busy at the oven, looking for all the world like she knew everything that had happened the night before, and her husband was sitting in the corner with a sort of ambiguous smile on his face, it seemed to the doctor.

"How could they possibly know?" he thought. "Ah, to hell with them . . ."

"You could have given me a shake," the doctor said a bit more softly, realizing that he was going to be driving all the way to Dolgoye with this fellow.

"Cain't worry someone who's sleeping. It's a pity." Crouper stood, holding his hat in two hands over his stomach.

"Of course it's a pity," said the miller's wife with smiling eyes, as she sipped tea from her saucer.

"What about the sled?" the doctor said, to change the subject.

"Fixed it. We'll get there."

"You wouldn't have a phone, would you?" the doctor asked the miller's wife.

"We do, but it doesn't work in winter." She dunked a sugar cube into the saucer and put it in her mouth.

"Very well, I'll finish my tea and come out," the doctor said to Crouper, as though dismissing him. Crouper left silently.

The doctor ate his blini, washing them down with tea.

"Tell me, this blackness, where'd it come from?" asked the miller's wife as she rolled the piece of sugar around in her mouth and slurped her tea.

"From Bolivia," said the doctor with distaste.

"From so far? How'd that happen? Someone brought it?"

"Someone brought it."

She shook her head:

"My, my. But how do they rise from the grave in winter? I mean, the ground is frozen through and through."

"The virus transforms the human body, making the muscles considerably stronger," the doctor muttered, glancing aside.

"Markovna, them's got claws like a bear's!" the worker suddenly said in a loud voice. "I seen it on the radio: they can crawl through earth, through the floor if'n they wants, like moles. They get through and rip people to shreds!"

Avdotia crossed herself.

The miller's wife set the saucer on the table, sighed, and also crossed herself. Her face grew serious and immediately seemed heavier and less attractive.

"Doctor, now you make sure to be careful out there," she said.

Platon Ilich nodded. His nose was red from drinking tea. He retrieved his handkerchief and wiped his lips.

"They's mighty vicious." The worker shook his head.

"The Lord is merciful," said the miller's wife, her chest heaving.

"Time for me to go," said the doctor, squeezing his fists and rising from the table. "I thank you for your hospitality."

He bowed his head slightly.

"Always welcome." The miller's wife rose and bowed to him.

The doctor went over to the coatrack, and Avdotia awkwardly tried to help him put on his coat. The miller's wife came over and stood nearby, her arms crossed.

"Farewell," nodded the doctor as he put on his fur hat and pulled the earflaps down.

"Goodbye," she said, bowing her head.

He walked out into the courtyard. The sled was already there, and Crouper sat holding the reins. Someone was busy in the barn, and the gates were open wide. The doctor looked at the sky: overcast, windy, but no snow.

"Thank God." The doctor took out his cigarette case, lit up, and began to settle in. Crouper waited until he was wrapped and buttoned up; then he smacked his lips and jerked the reins. Inside the hood the doctor could hear snorting and the already familiar clatter of tiny hooves. The sled set off and Crouper took hold of the steering rod.

"You know the road?" asked the doctor, inhaling the invigorating cigarette smoke with pleasure.

"There ain't but one hereabouts."

The sled moved slowly out of the courtyard, the runners squeaking.

"How much farther?" The doctor tried to remember.

"Roundabout nine versts. The road'll take us through New Forest, then there's Old Market, then there's fields—a baby could make it 'cross."

"Drive safely!" came a familiar female voice.

The miller's wife stood on the porch.

The doctor silently waved his hat, holding it by the earflap, which was rather awkward, and Crouper smiled and waved his mitten:

"S'long Markovna!"

The miller's wife watched them as they moved farther and farther away.

"She's an interesting woman, I have to admit," thought the doctor. "How quickly everything happened . . . But did I want it to? Yes, I did. And I don't regret a thing . . ."

"The miller's got hisself a good woman." Crouper smiled.

The doctor nodded.

"Luck, that's what," said Crouper thoughtfully, pushing his hat back off his forehead. "Like they says, 'On lucky days, even a rooster lays.' So there ye go: one fellow's kind and loving, but luck don't shine on him. Then some drunk with a foul mouth catches hisself a wife of gold."

"But how did that drunk manage to get the mill?"

"He got lucky."

"How so? The mill just fell straight from heaven?"

"Don't know 'bout heaven, but his papa, he's one of the little fellers, too, made hisself a fortune on taxes and bought that mill, and put his son in it. And that was that."

The doctor had nothing to add, and for that matter, he didn't feel like chatting with Crouper first thing in the morning.

"Markovna, she does all the work. He just shouts at everthin' in sight."

"Ah, to hell with him . . ." the doctor said, putting an end to the conversation.

Speeding along the riverbank, where the night before they'd trudged behind the broken sled, they passed willows and haystacks. They moved along smoothly at a clip, and the fresh, untouched snow whooshed softly under the runners. Soon, that same bridge appeared. Crouper kept to the left, turning onto the road. Though covered in new-fallen snow, it was quite discernible.

"How d'ye like that, ain't nobody passed by after us!" Crouper nodded at the road. "All gone and hid 'emselves from the blizzard."

"Maybe they drove by and then the tracks were covered."

"Don't look like it."

The sled moved swiftly along the road. Bushes, bushes, and

more bushes began to appear. The wind blew at their backs, giving the sled some help.

"Zilberstein is probably cursing me. But what could I do? There isn't even a telephone here. 'It doesn't work in winter!' Ridiculous! Nine—no, eight—versts now. Getting closer . . . I'll start the vaccinations straightaway, the delay won't matter . . ."

Before them a birch grove came into view.

"C'mon now, faster." Crouper clicked and whistled. "Get a move on."

The little horses increased their pace obediently.

They entered the grove at full tilt. Birch trunks lined the road.

"What a beautiful grove," muttered the doctor.

"Eh?" Crouper turned toward him.

"I said the grove is beautiful."

"Beautiful. If'n ye just chop it down."

The doctor chuckled.

"Why chop it down? It's pretty just the way it is."

"Pretty," Crouper agreed. "Won't last long. They'll cut it down anyway."

Snow began to fall, at first lightly, but by the time they'd passed through the birch grove, large flakes fell thick and fast.

"Wouldn't ye know it!" Crouper laughed.

The road led through a field, but there weren't any markers to be seen. Neither were there any traces of runners on the road. The field lay ahead, lost in the snowstorm; only here and there overgrown weeds or the rare bush stuck out.

They had driven half a verst when the sled slid into deep snow.

"Whoa!" Crouper pulled back on the reins.

The horses stopped.

"I'll go look for the road." Crouper jumped down, grabbed the whip, and walked back.

The doctor remained alone in the sled. Snowflakes continued falling in a dense veil as though they'd never stopped. Under the hood the horses snorted and stamped their hooves.

About ten minutes passed, and Crouper returned:

"Found it!"

He turned the sled around, leading it along his own tracks, while he tramped next to it, his legs plowing deep swaths through the snow.

They regained the road. But the doctor would never have guessed that this was a road; only Crouper could distinguish it in the snowy field.

"We won't go fast, yur 'onor, sir, else we'll up and drive off it!" Crouper shouted, wiping the snow off his face.

"Drive as you see fit," the doctor replied. "What about the runner?"

"Still holding. I nailed it together."

The doctor nodded in approval.

They moved slowly along the road. Crouper steered, gazing ahead. The snow thickened and the wind picked up, forcing the passenger and the driver to shield their faces.

The doctor sat with his collar pulled up and the rug all the way to his cheekbones. But the snow flew right into his eyes, under his pince-nez, and burrowed into his face, filling his nostrils.

"Damn it . . . ," thought the doctor. "They don't put up stakes to mark the roads . . . Could be a lawsuit if you think about it . . . Doesn't matter to anyone. Not the road authorities, the forest rangers, the patrols . . . What could be easier? Chop down a cart full of stakes in the fall, hammer them in every half verst at the least—though more often would be better, of course—so people can travel without worrying in winter. Swinishness, that's what it is . . . It's downright . . . obscene."

In front of them an endless, shapeless field stretched on, as though there were nothing else on earth, nothing but these miserable bushes and weeds.

"Slow going till Old Market, and then it'll be easier!" Crouper shouted.

"How does he see this road?" thought the doctor in amazement, hiding from the blizzard. "Professional instinct, no doubt . . ."

But soon they drove off the road again.

"Ay, damnation . . . ," said Crouper.

Once again he walked back, drawing a line in the snow with his whip. The doctor sat there like a snowman, buried in the blizzard, just brushing the flakes from his nose and pince-nez now and then.

Crouper disappeared for a long time; the doctor considered firing three shots from the revolver that lay in his travel bag.

When Crouper finally returned, he was completely exhausted, his jacket open at the chest, his face red.

"Well, did you find it?" asked the doctor, shifting and brushing bits of snow off.

"Found it," said Crouper, breathing heavily. "But almost got lost meself. Cain't see nothin'."

He scooped some snow off the sled and took a bite.

"And how will we make it?"

"Bit by bit yur 'onor, sir. God willing, we'll make it to Old Market. From theres on the road's wide, packed down."

Crouper smacked his lips. The horses reluctantly scraped their hooves against the drive belt. The sled didn't budge.

"What's the matter? Get yurselfs a bellyful at the miller's?" Crouper upbraided them.

The sled barely moved.

The doctor got down and banged on the hood in annoyance: "Let's go."

The horses snorted; the roan let out a piercing neigh. And the others neighed, too.

"No need to scare 'em," said Crouper, displeased. "They ain't scaredy beasts, thank God"

He jerked the reins and smacked his lips:

"There now, come along."

The sled strained. Crouper held the steering rod, leaned his other arm on the hood, and pushed. The doctor pushed against the back of the sled.

The sled started. Crouper steered it, but soon stopped and wiped his face:

"Cain't see a thing . . . Yur 'onor, sir, you go on ahead and follow my tracks, elsewise it ain't clear which way to go."

The doctor went ahead, following Crouper's tracks. The snow quickly covered them, and the wind blew straight in the doctor's face. The tracks stretched on ahead, and then began to bear right, going in a circle, it seemed to the doctor.

"Kozma! The tracks are circling back!" the doctor shouted, shielding himself from the wind.

"Means I went round and round out there," Crouper shouted. "Keep left and walk straight!"

The doctor bore left and suddenly fell to his waist in snow.

"Just figures . . . Damn it . . . ," the doctor mumbled.

As though mocking them, the wind blew harder, tossing snow in their faces.

"Now this . . ." The doctor stood up, leaning on Crouper.

"The devil pushed us into a gully!" Crouper yelled in his ear. "Quick, while the tracks are still there! There they are, just ahead!"

The doctor stepped decisively ahead, raising his legs high and pulling them out of the snow. The sled followed him.

The doctor walked on, keeping his eyes wide open behind his ice-coated pince-nez. Finally, just as he began to be truly exhausted and his fur-lined coat seemed heavier than a pood weight, he made out a track barely distinguishable in the snow.

"Tracks!" he shouted, but snow fell in his mouth and he began to cough, leaning into the blizzard.

Crouper understood and directed the sled along the tracks. They soon came out onto the road.

"Thank the Lord!" said Crouper, crossing himself when the sled was finally on hard snow. "Have a seat, sir!"

Breathing heavily, the doctor plopped down on the seat and leaned back, too weak to close his coat. Snow had filled his boots, and he could feel that his feet were wet, but he didn't have the energy to remove his boots and brush off the snow. Crouper covered him with the rug.

"We'll stand a tad, let the horses rest."

They stopped. The blizzard howled around them. The wind had gathered such force that it pushed the sled, causing it to sway and jerk like a living creature. The strong wind also blew the snow off the road, however, and the way was visible now—well traveled with hard-packed snow.

The doctor wanted to smoke but didn't have the strength to take his beloved, handsome cigarette case out of his pocket. He sat in a daze, his blue nose protruding between his hat and his collar, wishing with his entire being to overcome this wild, hostile, wailing white expanse that wanted only one thing from him—that he become a snowdrift and cease forever to desire anything at all. He remembered his winter doctor's visits to patients, but he couldn't recall a storm so intense that the elements impeded him. About three years ago, he got lost with the mail carriage, and he and the coachman lit a fire that night until a transport saw them and helped them out; and there was the time that he ended up in the wrong village, having driven almost six versts too far. But this was the first time he'd experienced such a powerful blizzard.

Crouper, no less tired than the doctor, dozed a bit. He remembered that before setting off he'd left the station boy to close the oven flue so the house would be warm when he returned. The house had warmed up, that was certain, but its master had spent the night elsewhere. He imagined his *izba*, unheated since morning, and Hoop, the hog, who would be hungry by now. He thought that if the boar squealed with hunger this morning, his neighbor, Fyodor Kirpaty, would think to look in and give him some feed. He thought about the clock ticking alone in the dark, unheated house. Or maybe the clock had already stopped . . . That's right, it'd stopped, of course, he hadn't wound it . . . He felt chilled and uncomfortable.

"Hey!" the doctor shoved him. "What are you doing? Sleeping? You can't sleep, you'll freeze."

Crouper turned and shook himself, coming to his senses. He began to shiver.

"Naw, I's . . . just resting up a bit." He took hold of the steering rod and tugged on the reins.

The horses moved without urging, apparently feeling the smooth road. The sled carried on.

The road went straight and, miraculously, the strong wind

bared it, blowing the snow into drifts on the side. Thus they crossed the field fairly fast and easily; but then the road sloped down and was lost in the snow. Crouper hurried and walked alongside. No sign of the road remained: in the hollow, the snow was equally smooth everywhere while the blizzard whirled and wailed above it.

"I'll . . . Damnation." The wind knocked Crouper down, but he held on to the steering rod.

The wind in the hollow blew so hard that the sled swayed. They lost the road right away and the sled halted in deep snow. Without a word, the doctor got down and walked on ahead through the snow. He found the road quickly; he tested it with his feet and kept going. Crouper followed in his path.

Slowly, step by step, they moved ahead. The doctor kept walking . . . He stumbled, sank into the snow, and staggered in the wind—but he didn't lose the road. The hollow went on and on. Suddenly, the doctor saw a hill coming closer, then realized that it wasn't a hill but some sort of whirling snow cloud, racing toward them. He crouched. Over his head flew an impenetrable vortex of snow; his pince-nez was torn from his face and fluttered on its ribbon.

"Lord Almighty, forgive me for my sins . . . ," the doctor muttered, falling down on all fours.

The tornado stormed by, and to the doctor it seemed like a vast helicopter of impossible size. The horses neighed in fright under the hood. Crouper squatted, too, but didn't let go of the steering rod.

This frightful thing passed over them and disappeared.

The doctor put on his pince-nez and looked at the rise ahead, the way out of the hollow. He saw the bared road.

"There's the road!" he shouted to Crouper.

But Crouper had already seen it himself. Pleased, he waved his mitten at the doctor: "Yep!"

They made it to the road, sat back down, and drove on. The sled emerged from the hollow onto a gently sloping hillock, and Crouper stopped abruptly: there was a fork in the road. He didn't remember this fork. In good weather he wouldn't have noticed it, he would have gone the way everyone did. But now he had to decide which way—right or left.

"Old Market is 'bout two versts from the grove," Crouper thought, pushing his hat back on his forehead, which was damp from sweat and snow. "That means it's real close by, prob'ly to the left, and the road on the right, now, must lead around to the meadow. The meadow here's a beauty, nice and smooth . . . So . . . we go left."

The doctor silently awaited the driver's decision.

"Left!" Crouper shouted, turning the steering rod to the left and giving the reins a jerk.

The sled edged to the left.

"Where are we?" yelled the doctor.

"In Old Market! We c'n rest up here, and afterward the road runs straight."

The doctor nodded joyfully.

Crouper had been in Old Market only twice: for Matryona Khapilova's wedding, and with his little brother, who bought a couple of piglets from the old man Avdei Semyonich, whom everyone called Fat Ass. But that had been in the fall and spring, not in the winter in a blizzard. Crouper liked Old Market: there were only nine households, all of them well kept and prosperous. The people there made a living by carving, threshing, and making counterweights. And their meadows were fine. Crouper and his brother and the piglets rode back by way of the meadows because the high road was muddy with the spring thaw. The smoothness and expanse of the Old Market meadows had impressed Crouper. But right now they were all under the snow.

The sled crawled across the flat land. Crouper remembered that just before Old Market there was a little grove, maybe linden, maybe oak.

"As soon as the grove shows up—Old Market's right there. We'll knock on a door to warm up. We'll sit an hour or so and move on. Not far now . . . ," Crouper thought.

Sensing a village, the horses quickened to a trot even though the road was beginning to disappear under the snow and was soon entirely gone.

"I'll have to change my boots right away . . ." The doctor wiggled his toes, which were wet and already beginning to freeze.

Crouper glanced back at the doctor. "The grove'll be comin' up now, and then Old Market," he said to cheer up the doctor.

The doctor looked spent. His nose and pince-nez stuck out comically from the snow-covered figure hunched over the seat.

"Like a snow woman . . . ," Crouper chuckled to himself. "The old elephant, he's tuckered now. Such bad luck he's got with the weather . . ."

They moved at a slow pace along the white fluffy desert, but the grove of trees didn't appear.

"Not a mistake here 'bouts, too?" Crouper thought, gazing into the storm with his eyelids forced wide open, though they drooped with exhaustion and threatened to stick together.

Finally the trees could be seen up ahead.

"Thank God . . ." Crouper laughed.

They reached the grove. The trees were huge, old. Crouper remembered very young trees with the first May leaves.

"Couldn't have growed up so fast." He rubbed his eyes.

Suddenly he made out a cross under the trees. Then another, and a third. They came closer. There were more and more crosses, sticking out of the snow.

"Lordy, it's a cem'tery . . ." Crouper exhaled, pulling back on the reins.

"A cemetery?" The doctor began furiously wiping his pince-nez.

"A cem'tery," Crouper repeated, dismounting.

"Well, where's the village?" muttered the doctor, staring at the tilted crosses around which the blizzard danced and twined as though teasing and mocking them.

"Huh?" said Crouper, bending away from the wind.

"I said, where's the village?!" the doctor shouted in a voice filled with hatred, for the storm, the cemetery, and that idiot birdbrain Crouper who had led him who knows where. He was angry at his wet toes freezing in his boots; at his heavy, fur-lined, snow-covered coat; at the ridiculous painted sled with its idiotic midget horses inside that idiotic plywood hood; at the blasted epidemic, brought to Russia by some swine from far-off, god-forsaken, goddamned Bolivia, which no decent Russian person had any need for at all; at that scientific, pontificating crook Zilberstein, who cared only about his own career and had left earlier on the mail horses without a thought for his colleague, Dr. Garin; at the endless road surrounded by drowsy snow-drifts; at the snakelike, snowy wind whipping ominously above them; at the hopeless gray sky, tattered like the sieve of some stupid, grinning, sunflower-seed-cracking old woman, which kept sowing, sowing, and sowing these accursed snowflakes.

" 'Round here somewheres . . ." Crouper turned his head this way and that, utterly bewildered.

"Why did you drive to the cemetery?" the doctor shouted angrily.

"Just did, yur 'onor, that's all . . ." The driver frowned.

"Haven't you been here before, you idiot?!" shouted the doctor, and began to cough.

"Sure enough I been here!" Crouper shouted, taking no offense. "Only it was summer."

"Then why the hell . . ." The doctor began to talk but the snow flew into his mouth.

"I been here, yes I have." Crouper turned his head back and forth like a magpie. "But I don't know 'bout the cem'tery, cain't 'member it at all."

"Drive, drive! Why did you stop?" the doctor shouted, and began coughing.

"Ain't sure which's the right way."

"Cemeteries are never far from the village," the doctor suddenly screamed, so loud that he scared himself.

Crouper paid no attention to the shout. He thought a moment longer, turning his head from side to side, then led the sled decisively to the left of the cemetery, into the field.

"If'n the fork was Old Market one way, and the meadows t'other, and the cem'tery's close by Old Market, then I went true. The fork musta been here but we missed it. Now Old Market'll be left, and then the meadows."

Having calmed down and recovered from his own shouting, the doctor didn't even ask why Crouper hadn't retraced his steps but had turned the sled left and was crossing the field.

"It's all right, it'll be all right," the doctor muttered, trying to cheer himself. "There are a lot of idiots in the world. And even more assholes."

Dragging himself through the deep snow, Crouper led the sled into the field. He was so certain of the direction that he didn't pay much heed to the gathering snowy gloom that parted reluctantly ahead of him. The sled moved along heavily and the horses pulled grudgingly, but Crouper just kept walking alongside, letting the steering rod go and lightly nudging the sled; he walked with such certainty that gradually the doctor, too, was affected.

"We'll be there any minute . . . ," Crouper mumbled to himself, still smiling.

And indeed—the contours of a building soon appeared ahead of them in the whirling snow.

"We made it, doctor, sir!" The driver winked at his passenger.

Upon seeing the approaching house, the doctor was suddenly dying for a smoke. He also wanted to cast off his heavy coat and leaden hat, remove his wet boots, and sit down in front of a fire.

Crouper desperately wanted a drink of kvass. He blew his nose into his sleeve and walked along calmly, letting the sled move ahead of him.

"Who lives on the outskirts?" Crouper tried to remember, though there was no point in it since the only Old Marketers he knew were Matryona, her husband, Mikolai, and old Fat Ass. "Matryona's house is the third on the right, and Fat Ass's is next door to Matryona's . . ."

He glanced at the approaching building from under his hat, and his heart skipped a beat: this wasn't an *izba*. It wasn't even a drying barn or a hayloft. It didn't look like a bathhouse either.

The sled drove up to a dark-gray tent with a pointed top. On the surface of the tent was the image of a *living*, slowly blinking eye, an image familiar to both the driver and the passenger.

"Mindaminters!" exclaimed Crouper.

"Vitaminders!" said the doctor.

The sled arrived at the tent and stopped.

Crouper followed it. The doctor turned, stepped down, and shook off the snow. The wind carried the faint odor of exhaust. Then they heard an expensive gasoline generator at work inside the tent.

"So where's your Old Market?" the doctor asked, without anger this time, because he was happy that the lifeless white expanse had finally afforded him an encounter with civilization.

"Roundabout near here somewhere . . . ," Crouper muttered, looking at the smooth, taut, zoogenous felt of the tent.

He noticed a felt door, and knocked on it with his mitten. Inside, an iridescent signal floated up immediately. A felt window opened in the door and a narrow-eyed face and chewing mouth appeared:

"Whaddya want?"

"We got lost. We're lookin' fer Old Market."

"Who?"

"Me, and the doctor here. We're on our way to Dolgoye."

The face disappeared and the window closed.

"Vitaminders," said the doctor, shaking his head, with a tired chuckle. "Just our luck to meet up with them."

But he was pleased: the smooth, sturdy tent, standing firm in the wind, evinced the victory of humanity over the blind elements.

A few long minutes passed and the door finally opened.

"Please enter."

A thickset Kazakh gestured invitingly. It was obvious that they'd interrupted his meal, though, and that he wasn't very happy about it.

The doctor and Crouper entered a space that was dimly lit by electric lights and well heated. Two enormous violet Great Danes with sparkling bells on their collars immediately rose from their beds and moved toward them, growling. The dogs' violet eyes stared at the newcomers, and white teeth sparkled in their snarling pink mouths.

"Shoo!" the Kazakh shouted at the dogs, as he closed the door.

With low growls, the dogs went back to their beds. Nearby were two large gasoline snowmobiles, clothes hung on hooks, and numerous pairs of shoes in neat rows. This was the entryway of the tent. The smell of expensive, precious gasoline, the two snowmobiles, and the two sleek Great Danes had a calming effect upon the doctor, but Crouper felt intimidated. "Take your coats off, make yourselves at home." The Kazakh bowed slightly to the doctor.

The doctor began undressing and the Kazakh set about helping him.

"My littl'uns need to warm up a tetch." Crouper took off his hat timidly and smoothed down his soaking-wet hair.

"I'll ask the bosses in a minute," replied the Kazakh unflappably, as he continued assisting the doctor.

He helped the doctor pull off his boots and gave him a pair of felt slippers. A Kazakh servant girl wearing a long, brightly colored dress and an embroidered skullcap entered, pulled back a thick curtain with her thin hand, and gestured for the doctor to enter:

"Please, this way."

The doctor stepped through the opening. Crouper remained standing near the door, hat in hand.

It was brighter and even warmer inside the tent. The large round space with gray walls of the same zoogenous felt gave off a feeling of nomadic comfort as well as the sharp aroma of eastern incense. In the center of the tent, right under the roof vent, three men held court at the traditional low black square table of the Vitaminders. The fourth side of the table was empty. Seven servant girls sat along the wall to one side. The eighth, who had invited the doctor into the tent, quietly took her place with them.

The three men looked at the doctor.

"District doctor, Garin," said Platon Ilich, nodding at them.

"Bedight, Lull Abai, Slumber," the Vitaminders introduced themselves, bowing their shaved heads in turn.

Bedight and Slumber had European faces, but Lull Abai was distinctly Asian looking.

"You've appeared like an angel from heaven." The thin, narrow-cheeked Bedight smiled.

"In what sense?" The doctor smiled, wiping his foggy pince-nez.

"We are in desperate need of your help," Bedight continued.

"Is someone ill?" asked Platon Ilich, casting his gaze about.

"Ill." Slumber, who had a strong, thickset body, and a simple, almost peasant face, nodded.

"Who is it?"

"Over there." Bedight nodded. "Our friend Drowsy."

The doctor turned around. Something lay wrapped in a rug between two of the girls. The girls unfolded the rug and the doctor saw a fourth Vitaminder: he wore a gold collar inset with sparkling superconductors, and his head was shaved. Drowsy's skull showed numerous abrasions and bruises, and his face was slightly swollen.

The doctor approached him cautiously and looked at him without bending over:

"What happened?"

"He was beaten," answered Bedight.

"Who did it?"

"We did."

The doctor looked at Bedight's intelligent face.

"Why?"

"He lost some expensive things."

The doctor sighed disapprovingly, squatted, and took the battered Vitaminder's wrist. There was a pulse.

"But he's alive," said Lull Abai, stroking his thin beard.

"He's alive," said the doctor, as he touched the Vitaminder's face, "but he has a fever."

"A fever." Slumber nodded.

"That's the ding-a-ling," said Bedight, licking his thin lips. "But we don't have any medicines."

"And this is a matter for the law, gentlemen." The doctor's lower lip pursed as he looked at the beaten man.

"It is a matter for the law," Bedight concurred, and the other two Vitaminders nodded their shaven heads in agreement. "But we are counting on your understanding."

"I'll have to report it," said Platon Ilich rather indecisively, realizing that in saying these words he might end up back out in the discomfort of the wailing blizzard.

"We will thank you," said Lull Abai, pronouncing the Russian words carefully.

"I don't take bribes."

"We won't thank you with money," Bedight explained. "We'll let you try a sample."

The doctor looked at Bedight silently.

"A sample of our new product."

Platon Ilich's eyebrows climbed upward and he took off his pince-nez to wipe it. The doctor's nose was pink from the warmth.

"Well . . ." He pushed his pince-nez up on the bridge of his nose, sighed, and slowly shook his head.

The Vitaminders sat motionless, waiting.

"Of course, it's hard . . . to refuse." The doctor exhaled, overcome by a rush of helplessness. He reached for his handkerchief with a sense of doom.

"We were beginning to fear that you would refuse." Bedight grinned.

The Vitaminders laughed. The servant girls laughed quietly.

The doctor blew his nose with a honk. Then he laughed as well.

The Kazakh's well-fed face appeared from behind the curtain:

"Masters, the driver is asking to warm his horses."

"How many are there?" asked Slumber.

"Don't know. They're little ones."

"Ah, little ones . . ." Slumber glanced at Bedight.

"Build them a shed," ordered Bedight. "And give him something to eat."

The Kazakh withdrew.

"In that case . . . I . . . need my traveling bags . . . ," the doctor muttered, leaning over Drowsy's beaten body again. "And I need to wash my hands with soap."

He was ashamed of his weakness, but couldn't help himself: he'd sampled the Vitaminders' products when means permitted. They made the life of a provincial doctor much easier. He allowed himself to indulge at least once every two months. But in the last year his finances had been worse, much worse: his already modest salary had been cut by eighteen percent. He'd had to refrain, and so it had been a year since Dr. Garin had *shone*.

He was ashamed of his weakness, and he was also ashamed of his shame, and then ashamed of this double shame. He became indignant and cursed himself abruptly and furiously:

"Idiot . . . Bastard . . . Damned hypocrite."

His hands trembled. He had to occupy them with something, so he began to unfold the rug, fully exposing the figure lying there. The Vitaminder moaned.

Meanwhile, two girls had brought the travel bags, wiped the snow off them, and set them by the doctor. Two others brought him a pitcher of water, a basin, and a towel.

"And the soap?" asked Platon Ilich, taking off his jacket and rolling up his shirtsleeves.

"We don't have soap," replied Bedight.

"No? What about vodka?"

"We don't keep any of that swill."

"Ah, I have some alcohol . . . ," the doctor remembered.

Opening his travel bag, he took out a round bottle, splashed water on his hands, wiped them with the towel, and then washed them in alcohol.

"Let's see now . . ." The doctor unbuttoned Drowsy's shirt, put his stethoscope to the man's chest, and began to listen, his eyebrows raised.

"We didn't beat him on the heart," said Lull Abai.

"His heart's fine," concluded the doctor.

He examined the Vitaminder's limbs. The man moaned again.

"His arms and legs are in one piece."

"We beat him on the stomach and the head," said Slumber.

The doctor pulled up the shirt, revealing the Vitaminder's stomach. He palpated it, concentrating, his red nose hanging over the man. The man kept on moaning.

"No swellings or internal injuries," said the doctor, pulling the shirt down and leaning over the head. "But here it looks like we have a concussion. Has he been unconscious a long time?"

"Since yesterday."

"Any vomiting?"

"No."

The doctor put smelling salts under the man's nose:

"Come on now, my good fellow."

The Vitaminder frowned slightly.

"Can you hear me?"

A weak moan came in reply.

"Hold on just a minute now. Be patient," the doctor comforted.

Garin took out a hypodermic and an ampoule; he rubbed the Vitaminder's tattooed shoulder with alcohol and gave him a shot.

"It'll get better." He removed the hypodermic.

"Why did you roll him up in a rug?" the doctor asked.

The Vitaminders looked at one another.

"To calm him down," Slumber answered.

"Like in a cradle." Bedight yawned.

"We rubbed sheep fat on the soles of his feet, too," said Lull Abai.

The doctor didn't comment on that bit of information.

After the shot, Drowsy's cheeks grew rosier.

"Can you move your arms and legs?" asked the doctor in a loud voice.

Drowsy moved his arms and one leg.

"Wonderful. Consequently—we know his spine is intact . . . What hurts?"

The blood-caked lips opened:

"Huh-huh . . ."

"What?"

"He-he-hed."

"Your head hurts?"

"Uh-huh."

"A lot?"

"Uh-huh."

"Dizzy?"

"Uh-huh."

"Nauseous?"

"Uh-huh."

"Liar . . . Liar!" Slumber cried. "He hasn't barfed once all this time."

The doctor looked at Drowsy's head:

"No fractures. Only bruises. The neck is all right."

He retrieved some iodine and applied it to the abrasions on the man's face. Then he applied calendula lotion.

"Metalgin-plus and rest," said the doctor, straightening up. "And warm liquid nourishment."

Bedight nodded in understanding.

"We were afraid he'd die," said Lull Abai.

"No danger to his life."

The Vitaminders smiled in relief.

"Well now, just like I said!" Bedight grinned. "Do you have any Metalgin?"

"I'll leave you five tablets."

"We thank you, doctor," said Slumber, inclining his head.

The doctor took out a pack of Metalgin-plus, punched out one tablet, and gestured to the servant girl:

"A glass of water."

The girl poured some water. The doctor placed the tablet in the patient's mouth and held the cup for him to sip. The patient began to cough.

"Calm down. The worst is over . . . ," the doctor comforted him.

He held his hands over the basin. The girl poured water over them. The doctor dried his hands and rolled down his shirtsleeves:

"That's it."

The doctor's heart pounded in anticipation. But he made an effort to look calm.

"Have a seat," said Bedight, nodding toward the empty place at the square table.

The doctor sat down, tucking his legs under him.

"The product!" commanded Bedight.

Two of the young women sitting by the felt wall opened a flat trunk and removed a transparent pyramid from it. It was exactly the same kind that had broken the runner on Crouper's sled on the snowy road yesterday.

"So that's what it was!" thought the doctor.

He now realized just *what* the Vitaminder wrapped in the rug had lost and why he'd been beaten.

"And he didn't lose just one . . . probably an entire case. That's a whole fortune . . ."

The doctor looked at the pyramid, which the girl carefully placed in the middle of the table. He had tried the Vitaminders' two previous products: the sphere and the cube. They weren't transparent, and were half the size of the pyramid.

"Why didn't I realize that it must be a product? Idiot . . . It was too strong. That confused me . . . Yes, that's what confused me. But there must have been an entire case of it lying about on the road. A year's worth of my salary. That's insane!"

The doctor grinned.

"You already had a try?" asked Slumber, not understanding the doctor's smile.

"No, of course not. I just . . . I've only tried the cube and the sphere."

"Everyone's tried them." Lull Abai shrugged his beefy shoulders.

"This is a totally new, fresh product," said Bedight, winking at the pyramid. "We're still trying it out ourselves. Looking for *the limit.* Getting ready for the spring."

The doctor nodded nervously.

"I should come back from Dolgoye by the same road . . . ," he thought cautiously.

Bedight pushed a button on the tabletop. A gas burner flared under the pyramid.

"It doesn't vaporize right away," explained Slumber.

"Not like the cube and the sphere?" Excited, the doctor sniffed and licked his lips.

"No. The entire thing has to heat evenly. About four minutes."

"We can wait four minutes!" the doctor laughed nervously, dropping his pince-nez.

"Four minutes." Bedight smiled.

"Four men for four minutes." Lull Abai's face dissolved into a smile.

Meanwhile, Crouper was eating hot noodles with chicken, sitting in a separate shed that had been built just for him. He'd never before seen how things were constructed out of zoogenous felt. The Vitaminders' servant, the Kazakh, Bakhtiyar, demonstrated the whole process to Crouper with an air of superiority. First he told him to move the sled as close as possible to the wall of the tent; then he stuck three long rake-like *combs* into the snow, to delineate the perimeter of the shed; and then, putting on protective gloves, he squirted a tube of zoogenous felt paste onto the combs, applied "Living Water" spray, and looked triumphantly at Crouper. Crouper stood there with his birdlike grin, one hand on the sled as though afraid to lose it. The gray paste stirred, and felt fabric began to grow from it fiber by fiber. Despite the snow, three felt walls grew until they surrounded the sled and its owner. Bakhtiyar stood outside.

"Well?" Bakhtiyar asked smugly.

"Handy," replied Crouper in amazement.

"Technology."

"Tek-nol-logy," Crouper repeated in a voice full of cautious respect.

As soon as the felt walls had reached Bakhtiyar's height, he grabbed the "Dead Water" spray and sprayed the sides of the walls. The felt stopped growing. The Kazakh drove a comb into the top edge of the largest wall, sprayed a bit of "Living Water" on it, and the shed roof began to grow. Inside the room, Crouper crouched on the sled's seat; watching the roof crawl across overhead, he grabbed the steering rod and reins for some reason. The roof kept going until it reached the opposite wall and completely covered the shed. Crouper and the horses were separated from the storm, the cold, and the light of day. It was pitch-dark and unusually quiet.

Crouper could barely hear the Kazakh spray the "Dead Water" to stop the growth of the roof. Then everything was totally quiet. The horses, sensing that something unusual was happening, stood stock-still.

"How's it goin' in there?" Crouper knocked on the hood. The roan neighed. Then the three inseparable black bays neighed; then the buckskins; then the sorrels, then the grays, and finally— the slow chestnuts.

Another five minutes passed, and the sharp sound of an electric knife pierced the darkness. The Kazakh deftly cut a low door in the shed wall and pulled it aside, letting light and warmth in:

"Scared ya?"

"Naw." Crouper squirmed on the seat.

"Stay. I'll bring some chow."

Crouper remained sitting.

Bakhtiyar returned with a bowl of noodles and a spoon:

"Orders to feed ya."

"Thank you kindly," said Crouper with a bow of the head.

Though the shed was quite dark, Crouper could see a chicken wing in the noodles. He dug in with pleasure. Sensing that their owner was eating, the horses snorted and whinnied.

"Now, now!" Crouper reprimanded them, knocking on the hood with the spoon. "You still gots a ways to go, it's no time for food . . ."

The horses quieted down. Only the rabble-rousing roan neighed in displeasure.

"Just wait, ye red rascal . . . ," Crouper muttered fondly, chewing the tasty chicken.

He gnawed at the wing and then began chewing on the bone.

"Good folks," he thought, beginning to sweat from the hot food. "Even though they're Vitaminders . . ."

The transparent pyramid emitted a delicate whistling sound, and evaporated. The burner went out. At the same moment, a translucent half sphere enclosed the four at the table, separating them from the rest of the world; the sphere was of a zoogenous plastic so delicate that only the sound of its closing, reminiscent of an impossibly large soap bubble popping or the sleepy parting of a giant's moist lips, betrayed its existence.

"Madagascar," said Bedight, his enfeebled mouth slurring the traditional greeting of practicing Vitaminders.

The doctor wanted to reply "Racsagadam," but he plunged immediately into another space.

A gray, overcast sky. Occasional snowflakes. Falling from the gray clouds. Falling, falling. A damp winter smell. Or perhaps a thaw? Or early winter. A slight breeze carrying the smell of smoke. No. That's the smell of a fully stoked bathhouse. A pleasant smell. Burning birch wood. He moved his head. And heard a dull splash. Near the nape of his neck. He looked down. There was liquid, right near his face. Not water. Thick, with a familiar smell. A very, very familiar smell. But too thick. Sunflower oil! He's up to his neck in oil. He's sitting in some vessel filled with sunflower oil. It's a black cauldron, a large black cauldron with thick sides. There's a huge plaza around the cauldron. A square filled with people. So many of them! Hundreds, hundreds. They're packed together. What a huge, enormous plaza. Buildings line the sides of the plaza. European buildings. And there's a huge cathedral. He's seen that cathedral somewhere before. Prague, probably. It looks just like it. Yes, that's it, Prague.

Although, maybe it isn't Prague. Warsaw? Or Bucharest? Kraków? No, it's probably Warsaw. The main square. And there are hundreds and hundreds of people in the square. They're all staring at him. He wants to move, but he can't. He's tied up. Tied with a thick rope. Tied as though he were in the womb. His knees bent, pressed to his chest, pulled up by the rope. His hands are tied to his ankles. He moves his fingers. They're free. He touches the soles of his feet. His wrists are firmly bound to his ankles. He's sitting on the bottom of the cauldron. He's touching the bottom. He's like a buoy. That's how he learned to swim. When he was a boy he pretended to be a buoy. That was a long time ago. On a wide river. It was sunny and warm. His father stood on the shore in a broad straw hat. His father laughed, and his glasses shone in the sun. He pretended to be a buoy and watched his father. Two horses stood on the shore and drank from the river. A naked boy sat on one horse and looked at him disdainfully. But he pretended to be a buoy. That was a long time ago. A very long time ago. And now he's tied up. In this cauldron. The cauldron is raised. It's on a platform. The edge of the platform is framed with thick logs. He can see them. The thick black edge of the cauldron blocks the view of most of the platform. The cauldron rests on something. And two thick chains run through the eye rings of the cauldron to two freshly hewn posts. The chains are wrapped around these posts. Exactly four times. And fastened to them with huge, wrought-iron nails. The posts are also on the platform. Beyond the platform is the crowd. Everyone is looking at him. A lot of people are smiling. In the distance, near the cathedral, something is being read aloud quite solemnly, almost sung. Latin? No. Polish. No, it's not Polish. Some other language. Serbian? Or Bulgarian? Romanian! Most likely Romanian. They're reading something. Reading with great solemnity. In a slight singsong. They're reading something about him in a singsong voice! And everyone is listening. Everyone is looking at him. They're reading something about him. They're reading something about him alone. It is all about him. They read for a long time. He tries to scoot forward to the edge of the cauldron so he can lean his chin on it and pull himself up. But he suddenly realizes that the rope around his ankles and wrists is also attached to the bottom of the cauldron and is keeping his body centered in it. The rope is drawn through a ring on the bottom of the cauldron, right under him. He touches the ring with his fingers. It's a smooth half circle. A thick rope runs through it. He realizes that there's no way he can get out of this cauldron. Even with his hands and feet still tied. The ring won't let him. Terrified, he screams. The crowd laughs and hoots at him. People show him horns and give him the finger. The women are holding children. The children laugh and make fun of him. He jerks with all his might. For a moment he loses consciousness from the horror of it all. But he comes to when he begins to choke on the disgusting, stinking oil. He has oil in his mouth and nose; he coughs, coughs horribly. What vile vegetable oil! It stinks. There's so much of it. It's easy to choke on it. It laps thickly around his body. His grandmother used to pour this oil on sour cabbage. There's so much of it! The smell is overpowering. Only a slight breeze keeps him from suffocating. The smell makes him dizzy. Here and there, large snowflakes fall into the oil and disappear. They fall and disappear. Fall and disappear. How lucky they are. They aren't tied down to anything. They don't owe anyone anything. And now the reader shouts the last word in a loud, triumphant voice. The crowd roars. It roars and people raise their fists. It roars so loud that the roar reverberates in the cauldron and causes faint ripples to form next to the cast-iron edges. Now someone climbs onto the platform. An adolescent boy holding a torch. He's wearing a suede jacket with copper buttons, red pants, and red shoes with turned-up toes. His face is beautiful, the face of an angel. Long chestnut hair falls to his shoulders. The adolescent wears a red beret with an eagle feather on his head. He lifts the torch high. The crowd cheers. He lowers the torch to the cauldron and leans forward. Only his beret is visible. The eagle feather trembles. There's a soft crackling sound that grows stronger. It seems to be tarred brushwood catching fire. The crackling gets louder. Dark smoke seeps out from under the cauldron. The adolescent leaves the platform. His beret and feather can be glimpsed in the crowd. The crowd roars and hoots. He makes one more desperate attempt to pull free, exerting himself so hard that he passes gas. The bubbles float up slowly around him. But the ropes don't give. He jerks, swallowing oil, coughing and gasping for air. The oil splashes around him. Stinking, viscous oil. But the cauldron is unmovable. It won't budge. He screams so loud that the echo of his voice reverberates against the cathedral and returns to him thrice. The crowd listens to him scream. Then it roars and laughs. He begins to cry and mutter that he is innocent. He tells the crowd about himself. He tells them his name. The name of his mother and his father. He talks about a terrible mistake. He has never hurt people. He talks about the physician's noble profession. He names all the patients he has saved. He calls on God as his witness. The crowd listens and laughs. He talks about Christ, about love, about the Gospels. And suddenly he can feel with his heels that the bottom of the cauldron is warm. He yelps in terror. Once again he faints for a moment. And again the oil, the stinking oil, brings him to his senses. He regains consciousness because he's swallowing oil. He's choking on oil. He vomits oil into the oil. The crowd laughs. He wants to tell them about his innocence, but he can't. He's gasping. He's coughing. He coughs so hard it sounds like shouting. The bottom of the cauldron is heating up. But the ring is still cool. It's thick and sticks out from the bottom. He holds on to the ring with his fingers. He clears his throat. Gathers his thoughts. Calms himself. Then he appeals to the crowd. He gives a speech. He talks about belief. He tells the crowd that he's not afraid of dying. Because he is a believer. He tells his life story. He's not ashamed of his life. He tried to live a worthy life. He tried to do good and to help people. There were mistakes, of course. He recalls a girl whom he made a woman, and who had an abortion. And he later found out that she could no longer have children. He remembers how, when he was a student and was at a party one evening in the dormitory, he got soused and threw a bottle out the window and hit a passerby on the head. He tells them about the time he didn't go to see a patient and the patient died. He lied a great deal in his lifetime. He gossiped and said spiteful things about friends and colleagues. He said nasty things about the woman he lived with. He sometimes begrudged giving his parents money. He didn't really want to have children. He wanted to live unencumbered, to enjoy life. It was largely because of this that he and his wife separated. He now repents his bad deeds. He spoke badly of the authorities. He wanted Russia to go to hell. He laughed at Russian people. He made fun of His Majesty. But he was never a criminal, he was a law-abiding citizen. He always paid his taxes on time. The bottom of the cauldron was getting hot. With tremendous effort, he balanced his feet on the ring. It was just a little warm. He held his own feet on the ring with his hands. He said that the worst thing in the world was when an innocent person was executed. That kind of death was worse than murder. Because murder is committed by a criminal. But even a criminal who commits murder affords the victim a chance to save himself. The victim might run away, grab the knife from the murderer's hands, or call for help. The murderer might miss or stumble. Or simply wound the victim. But when a person is executed, he has no chance of being saved. This is the terrible, merciless truth of the death penalty. He was always and still is an opponent of the death penalty. What is happening now on the main square of this town is even more terrible than the death penalty. Because the death penalty is being carried out against an innocent man. If they have all gathered here to carry out the death penalty against him, an innocent man, then they are committing a grave sin. And this sin will cast eternal shame on their town, and on their children and grandchildren. He feels the oil heating up at the bottom, and warm streams of it rising, displacing the cooler oil. The warm oil is crowding out the cold oil. And the cold oil moves downward. In order to heat up on the bottom, become warm oil, and rise to the top. He talks about the children standing here and sitting on their fathers' shoulders. The children are watching his execution. They will grow up and find out that he was innocent. They will be ashamed of their parents. They will be ashamed of their town. Such a marvelous, beautiful town. It wasn't made for executions but for joyous, prosperous lives. His heels slip off the ring and touch the bottom of the cauldron. The bottom is hot. He quickly pushes his heels off the bottom and grabs the ring and rope with the soles of his feet, and holds on to the rope. He talks about faith. Faith should make people kinder. People should love their brethren. Two millennia have passed since Christ's death, and people still haven't learned to love one another. They haven't truly grasped their kinship. Haven't stopped hating one another, deceiving, and thieving. People haven't stopped killing each other. Why can't people stop killing each other? If it's possible in one family, in one village, in one town, then isn't it possible in one country at the very least? The ring is heating up. His soles are feeling the heat. He jerks them away, but they immediately sink to the bottom. The bottom is even hotter. His feet recoil. But they can't just hang in the oil. They have to lean on something. His buttocks sink to the bottom and are burned. He puts his fingers under his buttocks and heels. Balances his fingers on the hot bottom of the cauldron. Then on the ring. The smoke from the fire billows around the cauldron and gets in his eyes. He closes his eyes and shouts that they are all criminals. That their town will be judged by an international tribunal. That they are committing a crime against humanity. That the international tribunal will sentence them all to jail. That an atom bomb will be dropped on their town. The crowd laughs and hoots. The oil is heating up. Hot streams float upward. They lick his spine like tongues of smooth flame. They lick his chest. There's no protection from them. They get hotter and hotter. The ring is already hot. He gathers air into his lungs. And screams with all his might. He curses the town. He curses the people on the square. He curses their parents and their children. He curses their grandchildren. He curses their country. He begins to sob. He belches forth all the curses he knows. He shouts obscenities, sobbing and spitting. The oil splashes around his head. He can't balance on the ring any longer. It's hot. Very hot. And the bottom of the cauldron is now horrendously hot. He can't even touch it. He pushes off the ring and floats in the oil. Pushes and floats. Pushes and floats. Plashes and floats. Plashes and splashes. He's dancing in the oil. Oil dancing! He begins to howl. Oil dancing! He howls, no longer addressing the crowd, but the roofs of the buildings around the square. Oil dancing! They're old tiled roofs. Dance! People live under them. Dance! Whole families. Splash! Women are making breakfast under those roofs. Plash! Children lean against their mothers. Splash! And sleep in their little beds. Children sleep, sleep, sleep. In their little beds. Little pillows, little embroidered pillows. Mothers embroider flowers on the pillows. Children sleep on the pillows. Sleep, sleep, sleep. And don't awaken. Sleep for days and days. You can sleep. For days and days. And not awaken. No one executes anyone for this. If you don't wake up. If you keep on sleeping. He shouts and begs to be awakened. He believes the children. He believes the pigeons on the tiled roofs. He loves pigeons. The pigeons can forgive him. Pigeons forgive everyone. Pigeons don't kill people. Will I die? Pigeons love people. I will die? Pigeons will save him. I'll die? He'll turn into a pigeon. I'll die? And away he'll fly. I'll die! The crowd begins to sing and sway. I'll die! What's that? I'll-a-die! A folk song? I'll-a-die! A song of this people? I'll-a-die! Of this wonderful people. Isle-a-die! Of this accursed people. Isle-a-die! This evil people. Isle-a-die! The people sing. Isledie! The people sing and sway. Isled! They desire his sublime death. Isled! But he'll turn into a dove and away he'll fly. Isled! No, it's the choir from *Nabucco*. Isled! They are singing. Isled and away! *Va, pensiero, sull'ali dorate!* Isled! And sway. Isled! They're singing. Isled! Swaying. Isled. Singing Isled! Swaying. Isled! Isled! Isled! Isled! Isled! Isled! Isled! Isled! Isled! Isled! Isled! Isled! Iled! Iled! Iled! Iled! Iled! Iled! I-l! I-l! I-l! I-l-! I-l! I-l! I-l! I-l! I-l! I-l! I-l! I-l! I-l! I-l!

The doctor opened his eyes. He was writhing in the arms of two servant women. His body was convulsing like an epileptic's. Nearby, the bodies of the three Vitaminders were writhing convulsively, too. The servants held them back carefully. The convulsions began to subside. All four of them gradually began to return to their senses.

The Kazakh girls wiped their faces, stroked them, and muttered soothing words in their own language.

"A superproduct," said Bedight, who had calmed down and taken a sip of water.

"Nine points . . . ," Slumber muttered, wiping his wet face and blowing his nose. "Maybe even nine and a half."

Lull Abai said nothing: he just shook his melon-shaped head and wiped the narrow slits of his eyes.

For several long minutes the doctor sat still, dumbfounded. His pince-nez hung around his neck; his nose seemed to have grown even bigger and hung imposingly over his lips. All of a sudden he stood up, crossed himself vigorously, and spoke in a loud voice: "Thank the Lord!"

And then he began to sob like a child. He fell to his knees, his face buried in his palms. Two girls approached and embraced him. But Bedight gave them a warning sign and they stepped back.

After sobbing awhile, the doctor took out his handkerchief, blew his nose noisily, wiped his eyes, put on his pince-nez, and stood up.

"How marvelous, we're alive!" he said.

He suddenly started laughing, waving his arms about, and shaking his head. His laughter turned into a giggle. He giggled and giggled, to the point of hysterics.

The Vitaminders smiled. And they, too, began to giggle; they fell off their chairs onto the floor, into the arms of the servants. Laughter tormented them for some time. Eventually they stopped laughing, calmed down, shook their heads, began to chuckle, and once again dissolved into laughter. The doctor suffered from the giggles more than the others; it was the first time he had tried the pyramid product. He writhed on the felt floor; he squealed and sobbed; saliva sprayed from his mouth; his hands flapped; he whined; he turned his head back and forth, shook his finger at someone, exclaimed, lamented, and giggled, giggled, giggled. His nose turned red, like a drunk's, and blood flowed into his trembling cheeks.

Bedight made a sign to one of the girls, and she sprayed water on the doctor's crimson face.

He gradually grew calmer and lay on his back, hiccupping. After he caught his breath, he sat up. The girl gave him some water. He drank and sighed deeply. He took out his handkerchief again, and again blew his nose and wiped his face. He put on his pince-nez. Looking seriously at the Vitaminders sitting at the table, he spoke:

"Brilliant!"

They nodded understandingly.

"How much?" the doctor asked, rising from the floor and straightening his clothes.

"Ten."

"I'll take two." He fished in his pocket for his wallet and took out all there was—two tens, a three, and the five promised to Crouper.

"Of course, doctor," Bedight smiled. "Zamira!"

The girl opened the chest and took out two pyramids. The doctor tossed the two tens on the black table. Bedight picked them up with slender, sensitive fingers. The girl put the pyramids into a sack and handed it to the doctor. He took it and shook his head energetically:

"Time for me to go, gentlemen."

"You're going to leave?" Slumber asked.

"Absolutely!"

"Perhaps you'd stay the night with us?" Bedight touched his left shoulder, and the girl rushed over and began to massage it.

"No! I must be off, off!" said the doctor with a vigorous turn of the head. "Time to hit the road!"

"As you see fit. But it's warm and comfy here." Bedight winked at the girls. "Especially at night."

The servant girls laughed and suddenly sang in chorus:

"Lull Abai, we'll say goodnight. With roses, Bedight. Lay thee down and sleep, Slumber!"

The Vitaminders smiled.

"Lay thee down and rest, Lull Abai!" the slenderest of the girls cried out in a delicate voice.

Lull Abai's round face grew even puffier. The Vitaminders' smiles seemed to urge the doctor on: he desperately wanted to get outside and leave this felt comfort.

"I thank you, gentlemen!" he said in a loud voice, nodding as he headed toward the felt door, which one of the young women opened in advance.

"Drop by on the way back," said Slumber.

"You may be assured!" the doctor muttered decisively, as he disappeared through the door.

The girl grabbed the doctor's travel bags and followed him.

In the entryway the servants helped the doctor put on his coat. Bakhtiyar appeared.

"Now, where's my driver?" said the doctor, turning his head and pulling his hat on.

"In the hut." Bakhtiyar gestured toward the opening cut into the felt.

The doctor looked in.

Crouper was dozing, sitting on the sled with his felt boots resting on the open hood. The little horses stood between his legs, chewing.

"Kozma! My dear friend!" the doctor exclaimed joyfully.

He was happy to see Crouper, the sled, and the horses.

Crouper woke right away, turned, and lifted his boots out of the hood. The doctor set down the package with the pyramids, embraced Crouper, and pressed him to his breast.

"Well, I . . . ," Crouper began to speak, but the doctor hugged him tighter.

Crouper froze, bewildered. The doctor stepped back and looked him straight in the eye.

"All people are brothers, Kozma," the doctor said seriously, and with some solemnity. He laughed joyfully. "I missed you, friend!"

"Well, I just caught a few winks here." Crouper looked away, smiling in embarrassment.

Bakhtiyar watched them with a smile.

"Did you think of me?" asked the doctor, giving the driver's emaciated body a shake.

"Uh, I thought ye was asleep."

"No, my man! No time to sleep now. We have to live, Kozma! Live!" He shook Crouper: "Are we off?"

"Now?" Crouper asked timidly.

"Now! Let's go! Let's go!" said the doctor, clapping him on the shoulder.

"Well, I guess we could go . . ."

"Let's go, friend!"

The horses, still chewing the oat flour Crouper had given them, lifted their heads and snorted, watching alertly.

"If ye say so, I reckon we'll be off . . ."

"I say so, friend! Let's go! We have to hurry to do some good for people! You understand me?" asked the doctor, clapping him again.

" 'Course I understand."

"Then let's be off!"

He let go of Crouper, who immediately busied himself with the sled and set to strapping down the travel bags.

"Hide this one way back!" said the doctor, nodding at the package with the pyramids.

Crouper stuck the package under his seat.

Bakhtiyar unbuckled the laser cutter from his belt and aimed it at the felt wall. A blue needle of cold flame sparkled, an unpleasant crack was heard, and foul-smelling smoke appeared. Bakhtiyar deftly cut an exit in the wall and kicked it. The piece of felt toppled over. The blizzard rushed into the shelter. The doctor ran outside. The blizzard whirled and whistled about him.

The doctor took off his fur hat, crossed himself, and bowed to this familiar, cold, white, whistling space.

"Heigh-yup!" Crouper's voice sounded muffled from within the shelter.

The sled slid through the opening, leaving the warmth of the felt shelter.

The doctor put his hat back on and shouted, spreading his arms wide as though to embrace the blizzard, like he had Crouper, and press it to his breast:

"Woo-hooo!"

The blizzard wailed in reply.

"Ain't settled down at all, yur 'onor." Crouper grinned. "Look how she's hootin' and howlin'."

"We're off, off, off!" the doctor shouted.

"You head straight that way—and you'll come right to the village!" Bakhtiyar shouted, hiding behind the shelter.

"Marvelous!" the doctor replied, nodding at him.

"C'mon now, have aaaat it!" Crouper cried out in a thin voice; then he whistled.

Having warmed up and eaten, the horses started off energetically and the sled raced across the field. This whole time the blizzard had neither intensified nor slackened: it blew just as before, and just as before, the snowflakes fell and visibility was poor all around. Crouper, who had also warmed up and eaten, and had even managed to snooze a bit, no longer had any idea which way to go, but he felt no anxiety on that score. Moreover, the doctor exuded such an aura of certainty and correctness that it immediately washed away any doubts or sense of responsibility that Crouper had.

He drove along, glancing at the doctor's warmed-up nose.

This large nose, which not long before had been freezing, blue, dripping, and so frightened that it hid in the beaver collar, now exuded confidence and exhilaration, triumphantly parting the foggy atmosphere like the keel of a ship. The change was so remarkable that Crouper felt joyful and a bit mischievous.

"Well now, our Dr. Elephant, he'll get us outta here."

The doctor kept clapping him on the shoulder. He didn't hide his happy face from the wind. The doctor felt wonderful. He hadn't felt this wonderful for a long time.

"What a miracle is life!" he thought, peering into the blizzard, as though seeing it for the first time. "The Creator gave us all of this, gave it to us unselfishly, gave it to us so that we could live. And he doesn't ask anything of us in return for this sky, these snowflakes, this field! We can live here, in this world, just live, we enter it like a new home, specially built for us, and he hospitably opens his doors for us, opens wide this sky and these fields! This is truly a miracle! Indeed, this is the proof of God's existence!"

He inhaled the frosty air with pleasure and thrilled at the touch of every snowflake. With his entire being he recognized the full power of the new product—the pyramid. The sphere and cube provided an experience of impossible, unattainable joy, something that did not and could never exist on earth, something that man dreams of in his most unusual and deeply hidden dreams: gills, wings, a fiery phallus, physical strength, travel across amazing expanses, love for unearthly creatures, copulation with winged enchantresses. The bliss of innermost desires. But after the sphere and cube, earthly life seemed squalid, gray, and commonplace, as though it were deprived of yet another degree of freedom. It was difficult to return to the human world after the sphere and the cube . . .

The pyramid, however, allowed earthly life to be discovered anew. After the pyramid you didn't just want to live, you wanted to live as if for the first and last time, wanted to sing a joyous hymn to life. And therein lay the true greatness of this extraordinary product.

The doctor touched the pyramids under the seat with his foot: "Ten rubles apiece. On the expensive side, of course. But worth it, worth that kind of money . . . Hmm . . . I vaguely remember the location. How many pyramids did that dolt Drowsy lose there? Five? Six? Or maybe a whole trunkful? They have *product* trunks, after all, each constructed specifically for its own product: one for spheres, another for cubes, and this one for pyramids. How deftly they're placed in the trunk—without gaps, like one monolithic piece. High-tech manufacturing. Could he really have lost a whole trunk's worth? How many would that be? Twenty? Forty? All lying there under the snow now . . . An entire fortune . . ."

"Here we are, yur 'onor, Old Market!" shouted Crouper.

The few *izba*s of Old Market moved toward them out of the storm.

"We'll ask the way now!"

"We'll ask, my man, yes we will!" The doctor gave Crouper a resounding slap on his padded knee.

The sled left the fields of virgin snow and drove onto the snowy village street. Dogs began to bark in the yards. They drove up to an *izba*. Crouper hurried to knock on the gates. The doctor, sitting in place, lit up and inhaled the smoke greedily.

No one answered for quite a while. Then a woman came out wearing a long sheepskin coat. Crouper spoke briefly with her, and, happy, returned to the doctor:

"I knew it, yur 'onor! We go as far as the little grove, and then there's a fork. Our way is to the right! It's a straight road from there, straight to yur Dolgoye, no turning anywhere! Only four versts!"

"Wonderful, my good fellow! Just wonderful!"

"We'll find the fork before twilight, and from there even a blind man could make it!"

"Let's be off, then! Let's be off!"

They settled in, wrapped their coats tight, and took off. Old Market soon ended. The road was lined with bushes; here and there a lone dark reed stuck up through the snow.

"Look at that!" said Crouper, shaking his head. "The villagers don't even cut the reeds. That's the life!"

He remembered how he and his late father cut reeds in the autumn, then tied them and covered the *izba*. Every year they covered the roof in reeds. And the roof was thick and warm. Then one time it burned down.

"Kozma, tell me, my good fellow, what is the most important thing in life for you?" the doctor suddenly asked.

"The most important?" Crouper pushed his hat up off his eyes and smiled his birdlike smile. "I cain't say, yur 'onor . . . The main thing—is that everthin's all right."

"What does that mean—'all right'?"

"Well, so's the horses are healthy, there's enough to buy bread . . . and so's I got enough firewood, and I ain't sickly."

"Well, then, let's say that your horses are healthy, you're healthy, too, you've got money. What else?"

"I don't rightly know . . . I used to think I might start me up some bees. At least three hives."

"Let's say you've got your beehives. What else?"

"What else would I be needing, then!" Crouper laughed.

"Is there really nothing else that interests you?"

"Don't know, yur 'onor."

"Well, what would you want to change in life?"

"In my own? Nothin'. We're just fine as is."

"Well, then, maybe in life in general?"

"In general?" Crouper scratched his forehead with his sleeve. "So there wouldn't be so many ornery people 'bout. That's what."

"That's good!" The doctor nodded seriously. "You don't like angry people?"

"No, sir, I don't. I'd go a whole verst roundabout to miss a man what's mean and nasty. When I come up agin' 'em—I get sick. Feel like throwing up, like I ate bad meat. Take that miller. Soon as I see him, hear him, I feel it comin' on, don't need to stick two fingers down my gullet. I don't understand, yur 'onor, how come some people gotta be so evil?"

"There's no such thing as evil people. Man is good by nature, for he is created in the image of God. Evil is man's mistake."

"Mistake? Awful lotta mistakes around. When I was a boy, couldn't stand to see no one whipped. I'd get whipped, well, all right then, I'd have a cry, and that's that. But soon as they put someone else over the bench I'd just get sick, almost faint. Once I growed up, too, whenever I sees a fight—makes me sick, like I got rocks in my stomach. Awful lot of bad mistakes, yur 'onor."

"Terrible, Kozma, terrible. But there's far more good in life than evil."

"I guess there's a bit more."

"Good, good is so important!"

"Good's important, 'course it is. Do good, and it'll come back twice over."

"Well put, Kozma! You and I are going to the end of the world in order to do good for people! And what a wonderful thing that is!"

"Sure enough, yur 'onor. As long as we get there."

They drove through the grove and arrived at the fork. Both roads—the one to the left that led into the field, and the other, which turned right toward some bushes—were high with snowdrifts and untraveled.

"There's our road!" Crouper turned the rudder decisively to the right, and the sled shifted with a slight squeak and moved along the snow-covered road.

The doctor noticed that it was already getting dark. He took out his watch. It was exactly six.

"How is that possible?" he thought. "How long was I at the Vitaminders? Could it really have been almost six hours? How many hours does the product last? I should ask them . . ."

The road ran past patches of underbrush. It was a decent road, no wider and no narrower than others, and packed down, so it was visible even in the deepening twilight. The blizzard hadn't slackened; it was just as strong as ever.

After the turn the snow blew straight at their faces. The sled slowed down.

Crouper steered, and the horses pulled, their hooves making a crunching sound inside the hood. The doctor looked straight ahead.

Soon it was entirely dark. There was no moon. But this didn't bother either the doctor or Crouper. They continued on their way, just as calmly and surely. The doctor felt that the blizzard itself was showing them the way, forcing Crouper to steer directly into the wind. Snowflakes flew out of the dark into the travelers' faces, and they just needed to keep heading in that direction, without turning.

"Drive into the wind, overcome all difficulties, all nonsense and foolishness, move straight on, fearing nothing and no one, move along your own path, the path of your destiny, move onward steadfastly, stubbornly. That is the very meaning of our lives!" thought the doctor.

The sled leaned to the left, its nose tipped downward into the snow, and it stopped. The horses snorted and whinnied.

"Now we've gone off." Crouper got down, stepped into the snow, and immediately sank in almost to his waist. "Tarnation . . ."

The doctor also got down and brushed off the snow.

"It's a gully!" Crouper shouted to him from the ditch. "Thank God we didn't fall in! Yur 'onor, gimme a hand to get outta here . . ."

The doctor walked toward him but sank down himself; groaning, he grabbed the driver's arm and pulled. They turned over and over in the snow, helping each other. First the doctor pulled Crouper out of the ditch, then, once out, Crouper helped the stumbling doctor. Rolling around and around in the snow, they grumbled and cursed; the doctor lost his hat, but Crouper grabbed it.

Once they had made it out of the gully, they sat in the snow, leaning against the sled, and rested.

"We'll be needin' to push the sled," Crouper said, asking the doctor for help.

"We'll do it!" said the doctor, energetically shaking his hat as he stood up. "Just show me how!"

Crouper pushed against the back of the seat and gave the horses the command to back up.

"Whoa now . . . back, back, back . . ."

The doctor pushed from the other side.

After four tries they managed to slide the sled out of the ditch. They rested a bit, then sat back down and drove on. The road ran along some bushes, then sloped downward and dissolved into the snowy darkness. It was completely impossible to make it out. Crouper got down and walked ahead, feeling for the road with his feet. The doctor picked up the reins and slowly steered after him. They inched through the dip and eventually made it out. And here Crouper lost the road. He walked around in circles, up to his knees in snow; he kept falling into ditches, tripping, falling, and getting up again. The doctor could barely see his figure in the darkness.

Finally, Crouper returned, utterly exhausted; he fell to his knees and embraced the sled:

"Lordy . . ."

"Well, what is it?" asked the doctor.

"It's gone an' disappeared, like the earth swallowed it . . ."

"What do you mean 'disappeared'? Where did it go?"

"God knows . . . The devil must be leadin' us on, yur 'onor . . ."

"Let me go and look for it."

"Wait up, yur 'onor, sir . . ."

But the doctor headed energetically into the snow-spitting blackness. First he decided to walk straight ahead of the sled. But after about thirty steps through deep snow he hadn't found anything resembling a firm road. He returned to the sled and went to the left. He immediately ran into bushes. The doctor walked around them and continued on, trying not to deviate from the direction he'd chosen. But bushes again blocked his path. He again skirted them. The snow became very deep, and the doctor fell down.

"Nothing!" He spit at the wind-blown bush and gave a tired laugh.

Exhaustion, darkness, and the blizzard had not deprived Platon Ilich of the extraordinary, joyous, and buoyant mood that he had acquired earlier in the day at the Vitaminders.

"What an adventure!" he thought, breathlessly stomping through the snow. "This will be something to remember. I'll tell Zilberstein, and he'll have to buy me a drink, the skinflint . . ."

He started to go around the bush but tripped on something and fell. His hat went flying. The doctor sat up and stayed put for a while, exposing his overheated head to the blizzard. Then he put on his hat and felt around in the snow. He had tripped on a large boulder.

"Glaciers . . . The great glaciers . . . They rolled across Rus, bringing stones with them. And a new era began for humanity: man took up the stone axe . . ."

Pushing against the boulder, he rose. He reversed direction, following his tracks. But he was soon off course and for some reason ended back at the boulder.

"I went in a circle," thought the doctor.

He spoke out loud:

"Why?"

Straining his eyes in the darkness, he picked out his tracks. Once more he followed the path he had just tamped down. And once again he arrived at the boulder.

"Nonsense!"

He laughed, removed his pince-nez, and for the hundredth time wiped it with his white scarf, which fluttered in the wind. Again he went around the mysterious bush. According to the tracks, it seemed that he had been going in circles the whole time.

"This can't be. How did I get to the bush in the first place?!"

The doctor remembered that he had gone around the bush to the right the first time. Moving away from the stone, he headed left. But there were no tracks leading to the bush. He spit and walked straight on. He soon ran into another bush, most unpleasantly. Its branches painfully snatched the pince-nez from his face.

"Damnation . . ." The pince-nez dangled from its cord; he grabbed it, went around the bush, and continued on.

Ahead was darkness, wind, and snow. There was no end to the deep snow underfoot. There was no road, nor any trace of people. He trudged through the snow a bit longer, and stopped. He could feel that his boots had filled with snow and his feet were very cold. He didn't want to return to that damned bush. He took a deep breath and shouted at the top of his lungs:

"Kozzz-maaaa!"

The only reply was the howl of the blizzard.

He shouted again. To the right he heard something that

could have been an answering shout. The doctor headed toward the voice. The snow was now so deep that he was literally climbing over it, wallowing about, backstepping, and sinking down again. Exhausted and breathless, he finally came to the sled. Motionless and covered with snow, it looked rather like a large snowdrift in the dark. A snow-dusted Crouper sat in it, shivering. He didn't react to the doctor's appearance.

The doctor almost collapsed from exhaustion.

"Didn't find a damned thing . . . ," he exhaled, grabbing on to the sled.

"Well, I found somefin," Crouper said, his voice barely audible.

"Where?"

"Over there . . . ," Crouper replied, without moving.

"Why are you sitting here?"

Crouper said nothing.

"Why are you sitting here?!" shouted the doctor.

"Just waitin' fer ye."

"Why aren't you moving, you fool! Let's go!"

But Crouper didn't move; it was like he'd turned into a snowman. The doctor pushed his shoulder. Crouper swayed and snow fell off him in pieces.

"Let's go!" the doctor shouted in his ear.

"Froze through, I am, yur 'onor."

The doctor grabbed him by the shoulders and shook him; Crouper's hat slipped down on his face.

"Let's go!"

"Wait a bit, I'll warm up a little . . ."

"What do I need to do, crack your head open? Decided to kick the bucket, have you, you idiot?"

Under the hood the roan whickered, apparently worried about his master. The other horses began to whicker as well.

"Let's go, you dimwit! Quick now!" said the doctor, shaking the driver.

"Sir, we shud get a fire goin', warm us up a little. And then go."

Quite unexpectedly, this statement had a completely calming effect on the doctor. He imagined the flames of a fire and immediately realized how cold he felt after crawling around in the snow.

"The temperature has dropped . . . ," he thought in passing.

He softened right away, let go of Crouper, wiped his frozen nose, and turned his head:

"Where would you start a fire?"

"Right here's where we'll start it," said Crouper, nodding vaguely to the side. He slid off the seat and straightened his hat. "There's bushes here, lotta bushes. I'll go and see what I c'n find."

Crouper disappeared into the whirling snow before the doctor had a chance to answer.

"Where's he going, the fool?" the doctor thought irritably, staring into the darkness; but he suddenly relaxed and felt overcome with exhaustion.

He climbed up on the seat, wrapped himself in the rug, and sat down, shivering. Everything swirled and howled around him. The doctor just wanted to sit still, without moving, or hurrying anywhere, or doing anything, even talking. His wet feet were cold. But he didn't have the strength to take off his boots and shake out the snow.

"I have alcohol," he remembered, but just as quickly remembered something else: "Drunks freeze more quickly. Mustn't drink, not a drop . . ."

He dozed off.

He began to dream of his ex-wife, Irina: she sat with her knitting on the spacious, sun-filled porch of the dacha they had rented on the Pakhra River. He had just come from town on the three-o'clock train. It was a short day, Friday. The weekend was ahead: he'd brought her favorite strawberry cake from town, but it was too big—huge, in fact; the size of the couch. He set the cake down on the green, sun-warmed floor of the veranda, walked around it along the wall hung with living photographs, and was headed toward his wife, when he suddenly noticed that she was pregnant. Obviously in the seventh or eighth month, for that matter—her belly filled his favorite dress, the one with little blue flowers; she was knitting something quickly, and smiling at her husband.

"What's this?!" He fell on his knees in front of her and embraced her tightly.

He cried with joy, he was so happy, so impossibly happy; he would have a son, he knew for certain that it was a boy, and his son would be there very soon; he kissed his wife's hands, those gentle, weak, helpless hands, and they kept on knitting, knitting, knitting, not reacting to his kisses; he cried with joy, tears were streaming onto her hands, her dress, her knitting. He touched Irina's belly, and suddenly understood that her belly . . . was a copper cauldron. He touched the pleasant copper surface, pressed his ear to the copper belly, and heard something gurgling inside, something beginning to hiss and burble pleasantly. The belly warmed up. He pressed his cheek to the warm belly and suddenly realized that oil was beginning to boil inside it, and that little horses would be cooking in that oil, and that when they were done, they'd be like fried partridges, and that he and his wife would set them out on Mama's silver serving dish and feed the horses to their long-since-grown son, who, it turned out, was sleeping in the attic at that very moment, and they could hear his loud, mighty snore, which made the dacha shake and the wood planks of the veranda tremble, tremble, tremble ever so slightly.

"Look, Platosha," said his wife, showing him her knitting.

It was a pretty, intricately knit horse blanket for a little horse.

"We're having fifty children!" his wife said joyfully and gave a happy laugh.

The dream fell apart from a sharp blow.

Platon Ilich had trouble opening his eyelids. The snowy dark continued to swirl around him.

There was a repeat blow. Crouper was cutting chips off the rounded edges of the seat back with an axe.

The doctor began to turn around and was immediately seized by the shivers, which made their way from his feet to his head. During the short nap his immobile body had stiffened from the cold. The doctor shook so hard that his teeth chattered.

"Just a sec . . . ," Crouper muttered, fussing about somewhere nearby.

The doctor moaned and shook as he gradually awoke. Crouper had hollowed out the snow next to the sled and started a fire.

"Come on, yur 'onor," he called.

Platon Ilich barely managed to slide down from the seat. He was shaking. Teeth chattering, picking up one leg and then the other with tremendous difficulty, he walked over and sat down in the snow ditch, almost in the fire. While he was sleeping, Crouper had found and chopped up a dry bush. After setting fire to the twigs and pieces of the seat back, he broke off deadwood and stuck it in the fire, covering it from the snowstorm with his own body. Gradually the fire grew to a blaze between the two squatting men. The blizzard tried to put out the flame, but Crouper wouldn't let it.

The wood caught fire, and the doctor stretched his gloved hands into the flames. Crouper pulled off his mittens and stretched out his large, ungainly hands as well. They sat like that, immobile, silent, squinting when the smoke got in their eyes. The doctor's gloves warmed up, his fingers got hot, painfully so. The doctor pulled the gloves off. That pain and the fire conquered the shivers. The doctor felt like himself again. He retrieved his watch and glanced at it: a quarter to eight.

"How long did I sleep?" he asked.

Crouper didn't answer; he continued breaking off pieces of brushwood and shoving them into the fire. Illuminated by bursts of flame, his birdlike face appeared to smile, as if everything was just fine. He didn't look very tired. His face even conveyed a sort of joy and grateful resignation to everything around him: the blizzard, the snowy fields, the dark sky, the doctor, and the fire flaring in the wind.

While the brushwood burned, the doctor and the driver warmed up. The energy the doctor had acquired at the Vitaminders returned to him; he was ready to drive on, to struggle with the storm. On the other hand, after sitting at the fire, Crouper was drowsy and in no hurry to go anywhere.

"Where's the road?" the doctor asked as he stood up.

"Right over there . . . ," muttered Crouper, his eyes half closed and his head down.

"Where?" The doctor couldn't hear him.

Crouper gestured to the right of the sled.

"Let's go!" the doctor commanded.

Crouper rose reluctantly. The wind had scattered the last

burning branches. The doctor wiped off the snow from the seat and was about to sit down, but, on seeing that Crouper was pushing the back of the seat to get the sled moving, he came around to help him.

"One, two, ooooooffff!" Crouper shouted in a weak voice as he pushed.

The horses barely managed to get going. The sled slid along so slowly it was as though there weren't any horses under the hood at all, just two men pushing a seat that had been chipped away by an axe.

"C'mon, c'mon! C'mon now!" Crouper shouted.

The sled didn't gain any speed. Crouper stopped pushing it, brushed the snow off the hood, and opened it.

"What is it?" he asked in a hurt tone of voice.

On seeing their master, the little horses whickered discordantly. From their voices it was clear that they were tired and half frozen.

"Ain't I fed you?" Crouper took off his mitten and petted the horses' backs. "Ain't I took care of you? What's this? C'mon, c'mon now!"

He gave the horses a push. They tossed their heads, bared their teeth, snorted, and looked at their master.

"Yur the only hope now, you good-fer-nothins," he said, stroking them. "Just got a teeny ways more to go, and here yur wantin' to loaf about. C'mon now, c'mon!"

He patted the horses on the back.

The doctor started doing exercises and waving his arms. Crouper leaned over under the hood, so that he was hanging right over the horses, his face almost touching them.

"C'mon now, c'mon!"

The horses raised their mouths as much as their collars would allow and started whinnying and grabbing at his face with their lips.

"Go on, tell me, tell me all about it!" Crouper grinned.

Friendly whinnying filled the sledmobile's hood. The horses stretched toward their master; frosty horse noses pushed at the man's cheeks and nose and tugged at the tufts of his thin beard. Crouper blew on them hard, as though pushing them away. But this just excited the horses even more. The roan, reaching back harder than the others, almost dislodging his collar, stretched his neck out, bared his teeth, and grabbed his master by the bridge of his nose.

"Ay, ay, ay," said Crouper, flicking him on the back.

The horses whickered.

"Now that's it, that's more like it," Crouper patted them approvingly. "Ain't dead, is ye? And none of that!"

Winking at the little horses, he closed the hood, straightened up, and clapped his gloves together to energize himself:

"Let's go, let's go!"

The doctor, breathing hard from his exercises, grabbed the back of the seat: "Let's go!"

Crouper ran around to the other side and grabbed the seat where the axe had nicked it:

"Let's goooo!"

The sled moved, crawling straight into the storm.

"Let's go!" roared the doctor.

"Let's gooooo!" Crouper croaked.

The sled moved across the snow like a cutter across water; Crouper guided it not so much by the barely distinguishable tracks as by his absolute certainty that the road was there, straight ahead, and that it couldn't be missed.

They drove onto the road.

"Sit down, doctor!" Crouper shouted.

The doctor jumped on as the sled gained momentum, and plopped down on the seat. Crouper pushed the sled a bit longer; then he, too, jumped on and settled down, holding the reins.

The sled drove along the snow-covered road.

Suddenly something happened in the pitch-dark sky, and the travelers could make out a field up ahead, bushes, a black strip of forest to the right, and to the left two huge trees standing alone in the field. They could see the snow falling on the landscape.

The doctor and Crouper lifted their heads: a bright but waning moon shone through a break in the clouds. They could see dark-blue sky between huge masses of gray cloud. "Thank God!" Crouper muttered.

And as though by some miraculous gesture of an unseen hand, the flying snow began to thin and soon stopped altogether. Only an intermittent wind blew snow across the field and road, and rocked the roadside bushes.

"It stopped, yur 'onor!" Crouper laughed, and poked the doctor with his elbow.

"It stopped!" the doctor repeated, with a happy nod of his hat.

Clouds still crawled across the moon, but they seemed weaker. They were quickly blown out of the sky. The stars twinkled, and the moon illuminated everything around them.

The blizzard had stopped.

The snowy road was visible now, the horses pulled, and the sled slid along, its runners whooshing through the freshly fallen snow.

"Looky how lucky, yur 'onor!" Crouper smiled, adjusting his hat. "The lucky man's rooster will cock-a-doodle-do, and lay him eggs, too." The doctor was so happy, he wanted to smoke, but he changed his mind: he felt good even without his cigarette. Everything was amazingly beautiful.

The clear night sky expanded above a huge snowy field. The moon reigned supreme in the sky, glinting in a myriad of recently fallen snowflakes and glimmering silver on the frost-covered matting of the hood; on Crouper's mittens, which held tight to the reins; and on the doctor's hat, pince-nez, and long fur coat. The stars twinkled like diamonds strewn high in the sky. A chill, faint breeze blew from the right, carrying the smell of nighttime, fresh snow, and a far-off human dwelling.

The previous joyful and overflowing feeling of life returned to the doctor; he forgot his exhaustion and his freezing feet, and took a deep breath of the frosty night air.

"The overcoming of obstacles, awareness of your path, steadfastness ... ," he thought, yielding with pleasure to the beauty of the surrounding world. "Each person is born to find his own way in life. God gave us life and he wants one thing from us: that we realize why he gave us this life. It wasn't simply to live without meaning, like a plant or animal. We were meant to understand three things: who we are, where we come from, and where we are headed. For example, I, Dr. Garin, *Homo sapiens*, created in his image and likeness, am traveling along this field at night to a village, to sick people, in order to help them, to safeguard them from an epidemic. This is the essence of my life, here and now. And if that shining moon were to suddenly collapse and life were to cease, then at that very second I would be worthy of being called a Human Being, because I didn't turn away from my path. How wonderful!"

Suddenly the horses whinnied and snorted, stamping on the drive belt. The sled slowed down.

"What is it?" Crouper adjusted his hat.

The horses stopped and snorted.

Crouper stood up and looked ahead. On the right, two shadows passed among the thin undergrowth.

"Not wolves?" Crouper jumped down into the snow, took off his hat, and looked closely.

The doctor couldn't make out anything in particular. But suddenly two pairs of yellow eyes shone in the bushes.

"Wolves!" Crouper exclaimed, waving his hat. "Oy, that's bad luck . . ."

"Wolves." The doctor nodded in agreement. "Don't be scared. I have a revolver."

"The horses won't go that way." Crouper put on his hat and whacked his mitten on the hood. "Oh, Lord, just what we needs . . ."

"We'll scare them off!" the doctor exclaimed. He jumped down from the sled, went around to the back, and began unfastening his traveling bag.

"Two more . . . ," Crouper said, noticing two wolves further off, to the left.

He looked straight ahead and could make out another wolf calmly crossing the moonlit field in the distance.

"Five!" he shouted to the doctor.

The wolves began to howl.

The horses snorted and neighed in fear.

"Don't ye be scared, I won't let 'em getcha." Crouper slapped his mitten on the hood.

The doctor finally unstrapped his snow-dusted traveling bag, brought it around, and threw it on the seat; he opened it, took out his small, snub-nosed revolver, and cocked the trigger.

"Where are they?"

"Thataways." Crouper waved his mitten.

The doctor took four steps in the direction of the wolves, but went off the road and plunged into deep snow. He grabbed on to some bushes and shot three times. Yellow flashes illuminated the moonlit plain.

The shots made the doctor's ears ring.

The wolves trotted off to the right, all five, one after the other. The doctor saw them:

"Now, you . . ."

He fired two more shots after them.

The wolves continued at the same pace. They soon disappeared into the bushes.

"There, now." The doctor stuck his revolver, still smelling of gunpowder, into his pocket, and turned to Crouper: "The path is clear!"

"The path is clear . . . ," said Crouper, fussing about, and opening the sled hood. "But the horses, now . . ."

"What about the horses?"

"They're afraid of the wolf smell."

The doctor looked over in the direction the wolves had gone. They had disappeared from the field.

"But their tracks are cold!" he said, shaking his hat. "What smell?"

Paying him no mind, Crouper threw back the matting. The horses stood silently inside the hood. Turning their heads, they looked at Crouper.

"Don't ye be scared none, I won't let 'em getcha," he told them.

They stood, staring, moving their tiny ears. Their eyes gleamed in the moonlight.

"What's wrong with them?" The doctor leaned over the hood.

"Let 'em stand a spell." Crouper scratched his head under his hat. "And then we'll be off."

"What do you mean, 'Let them stand'?"

"They had a fright."

The doctor peered at Crouper.

"I'll tell you what: don't play games with me. Had a fright! Am I supposed to dawdle about here all night with you?! Sit down right now! You get them going, damn it! Make it quick! Had a fright! I'll give you a fright! They've been standing long enough! Come on now, make it quick!"

The doctor's loud voice carried over the field.

Crouper obediently began to cover the horses.

The doctor sat down, placing his traveling bag at his feet; he touched the package with the pyramids—it was still there.

Crouper sat next to him, took hold of the rudder, gave the reins a jerk, and made a clucking noise with his tongue: "C'mon now, my lovelies."

It was quiet under the hood, as though it were empty. Turning to look at the doctor, Crouper clucked again:

"C'mon!"

Utter silence reigned under the hood.

"Are you mocking me?" asked the doctor impatiently. "All right, give me the whip! Open it up!"

He pulled the little whip out of the case.

"They won't go, yur 'onor, sir."

"Open it up, I told you!"

"Don't, sir. The wolves gets 'em all nervous-like. They won't move till they comes out of it. One time I hadda stand with 'em near Khliupin fer near on two hours . . ."

"O-pen up! Open it up!" the doctor shouted, and shoved Crouper.

Crouper fell off the coachman's seat, lost his hat, and floundered in the snow. The doctor jumped down awkwardly and began pulling the matting off the hood:

"Stand around and wait, will you! I'll teach you to stand around! People are dying, and he says we should wait!"

Holding his hat in hand, Crouper approached the doctor:

"Yur 'onor, don't do it."

"I'll show you—huh—stand and wait . . . ," the doctor muttered, pulling the frozen loops of the matting from the hooks.

He suddenly realized that it was Crouper, this aimless man, lacking all ambition, with his disorganized slowness and centuries-old peasant reliance on "somehow or another" and "with luck, everything will turn out," who was preventing them from moving directly toward the doctor's goal.

"You stinking asshole!" the doctor thought angrily.

Having pulled off half of the matting, he threw it back.

The little horses stood bathed in moonlight, looking like porcelain figurines. They stared at the doctor.

"Now I'll show you—get a mooooove on!" The doctor waved the little whip, but Crouper grabbed his hand:

"Yur 'onor . . ."

"How dare you?" The doctor jerked his hand away. "What do you think you're . . . ? Are you trying to sabotage . . . ?"

"Yur 'onor . . ." Crouper wriggled in between the doctor and the sled. "Don't hit 'em."

"You just . . . I'll sue you, you scoundrel!"

"Yur 'onor, don't hit 'em, they ain't ever bin hit . . ."

"You just—out of the way!"

"I ain't gonna move, yur 'onor, sir."

"Get back, asshole!"

"I ain't gonna."

The doctor threw the whip aside, drew back his fist, and punched Crouper in the face. Crouper fell helplessly into the snow.

"Beat me, but I ain't gonna let no one tetch 'em!" he shouted in such a downtrodden and desperate voice that the doctor froze, his fist raised in readiness for another blow.

"What am I doing?" The doctor stepped back, surprised by his own fury.

Crouper floundered in the snow, then he managed to sit up, leaning against the sled, and silently picked up his hat. His bird-like face was still smiling, the doctor thought. Crouper put on his hat and remained sitting.

It was surprising that there hadn't been a peep out of the horses.

The doctor sighed heavily, walked off a bit, retrieved a cigarette, and lit up.

Far, far off, a wolf howled.

"How stupid . . . ," the doctor thought. "I lost my temper. Why? Everything seemed to be working out, and the blizzard has stopped. But he doesn't want to move. Ridiculous!"

He remembered that the last time he had punched a man in the face was at home in Repishnaya, when they'd had to tie up three guys who'd eaten poison mushrooms. He'd had to hit one of them twice.

"And now here I am, back at it," the doctor thought, annoyed at himself. He threw down his unfinished cigarette.

The doctor walked over to Crouper and squatted. He put his hand on Crouper's shoulder:

"Kozma, don't . . . don't be mad."

"Why shud I . . ." Crouper grinned.

The doctor noticed that Crouper's split lip was bleeding. He pulled his handkerchief out and pressed it against Crouper's mouth.

"It weren't nothin', yur 'onor . . ." Crouper pushed his arm away and spat.

The doctor grabbed him under the arm to help him up: "Come on now."

Crouper stood up, leaning against the sled. He pressed his lip to his mitten.

"Don't be mad." The doctor clapped him on the shoulder. "I'm just tired."

Crouper grinned.

"We have to go," said the doctor, rocking Crouper's light body.

"That's sure enough."

"Well, then, why are we standing around? Let's be off."

"They won't move, yur 'onor. They gotta get over the willies."

The doctor was about to say something harsh and weighty, but changed his mind and tramped off in a fit of pique. Crouper stood there, spitting and touching his mitten to his lip; then he covered the horses and fastened the matting.

"They needs an hour to come out of it. And then we'll be off."

"Do whatever you need to."

The doctor sat down on his seat, wrapped the rug around tight, and shivered; only his nose and the sparkle of his pince-nez could be seen from under his hat. He was suddenly chilled and uncomfortable, and not simply from the cold. The optimism and energy he'd had when he left the Vitaminders had vanished. The doctor felt cold and disgusted.

"A pile of shit . . . ," he thought, thrusting his gloved hands into the deep pockets of his fur coat and feeling the cold revolver in his right pocket. "Our life is nothing but a pile of shit . . ."

"*Schweinerei!*" He spoke the German word aloud.

Crouper climbed up onto the seat and sat next to the doctor. He showed no bitterness or offense. There was just his swollen upper lip, which made his birdlike mouth look even funnier.

They sat that way for about ten minutes. The moon was still shining in the cleared sky, and the wind had died down. A frosty silence reigned. The only sound was that of the horses' hooves stepping about cautiously inside the hood.

"Maybe a drink?" the doctor asked himself out loud.

Crouper just sighed.

"Just a swig apiece?" asked the doctor, turning toward him.

Crouper sniffed:

"We ain't agin' it, yur 'onor. It's shiverin' cold, so why not?"

"That's true." The doctor nodded. Leaning over, he opened his travel bag, rummaged around in it, grunting, and pulled out a round bottle that contained rubbing alcohol.

He pulled the rubber cork out, inhaled, and raised his arm, looking at the moon through the thick glass: "To our health."

He took a large swig, placed his left hand to his lips, and slowly exhaled into the cold glove, which smelled of smoke from the fire. The alcohol burned as it moved down his throat, causing him to remember the copper kettle filled with boiling oil.

"*Va, pensiero* . . . ," he muttered, exhausted, as he drew the freezing air in through his nose. Then he burst out laughing.

Crouper looked over at him.

"Here, drink." The doctor handed him the bottle.

Crouper took it with both hands, leaned over, and slowly leaned back as he took a gulp. He held his breath for a moment, and sat stock-still. Then he grunted like a peasant, shook his head, and handed the bottle to the doctor.

"Good?" asked the doctor.

"Good," Crouper replied, breathing through his nose noisily.

The doctor closed the bottle and put it away in his travel bag. He squeezed Crouper by the wrist.

"Don't be mad."

"It's all right."

"I'm just tired . . . Sick of everything."

Crouper nodded. The doctor looked around glumly.

"You hurry up those horses of yours somehow, hear?"

"They'll go on their own soon. It's in the little ones' blood, yur 'onor. They're scared of dogs and wolves. And weasels."

"But the wolf tracks are cold!" the doctor exclaimed with a hurt expression.

"That's right, but the fright's still there."

"Not that much farther to go, anyway."

"We'll get there."

"There are very sick patients waiting for me," the doctor said without any hint of reproach. He retrieved his cigarettes.

Crouper raised the collar of his sheepskin coat, shivered, and grew quiet.

The doctor, on the contrary, felt a surge of energy and warmth after drinking the alcohol. It felt like a tropical flower had blossomed in his belly.

"Down to the last two!" He grinned as he showed Crouper his cigarette case.

Crouper didn't move.

The doctor lit up. The irritability and impatience had left him. He smoked and squinted into the snowy plain. His eyes teared up, but he didn't feel like moving and wiping them. He blinked, but the tears stayed in his eyes, making everything around him swim, and the corners of his eyes felt pleasantly cool.

"Why are we always hurrying somewhere?" he thought,

inhaling the cigarette smoke and blowing it out again with pleasure. "I was in a hurry to get to Dolgoye. What would happen if I arrived tomorrow? Or the day after? Nothing at all. The people who've been infected and bitten will never be people again anyway. They're doomed to be shot. And the ones who've barricaded themselves inside their *izba*s will wait for me one way or the other. They'll be vaccinated. And they'll no longer fear the Bolivian plague. Zilberstein won't be happy, of course. He's waiting for me, cursing me up and down. But it's not in my power to overcome this cold, snowy expanse with a wave of my hand. I can't fly over the snowdrifts . . ."

Finishing his *papirosa* slowly, he tossed the butt into the snow.

A cloud crawled over the moon, plunging the field into the dark of night.

"Sleeping?" The doctor poked the driver.

"Naw," Crouper answered.

"Don't sleep."

"I ain't sleepin'."

The cloud moved past the moon. The field brightened again.

Crouper felt warm and calm after drinking the liquor. He sat with his knees pulled to his chest, holding on to his sides, his hat practically down to his nose. He peeped out at the expanse of moonlit field. He no longer thought about his unheated house, he just sat there and looked. The doctor was on the verge of asking him about the horses, when and why they first became scared of wolves, how soon they'd come out of it and be ready to pull the sled, but he changed his mind. He, too, sat motionless, giving himself over to the absolute calm stretching all around him.

The wind had completely died down.

They sat like this for a while longer. Neither the doctor nor

Crouper wanted to move. Tufts of cloud crawled across the moon and moved on, crawled across the moon and moved on. Crawled across the moon and moved on.

The doctor remembered that there was still a bit of alcohol left in the bottle. He took it out and took two large gulps with a pause between. He caught his breath and handed the bottle to Crouper:

"Drink up the rest."

Crouper came out of his trance, took the bottle, drank the remainder obediently, and put his mitten to his mouth. Stashing the empty bottle in the travel bag, the doctor scooped some snow from the matting, put it into his mouth, and chewed on it. Warmth spread throughout his insides once again. He cheered up and felt a surge of energy. He wanted to move and do something.

"What do you say, my good fellow, let's be off!" The doctor clapped Crouper on the shoulder. "Can't stay here forever."

Crouper got down, turned back the matting, and looked inside the hood. The horses looked at him.

"Let's go," Crouper said to them.

Hearing these familiar human words, the horses neighed discordantly. Nodding in approval, Crouper covered them, sat down, and tugged on the reins:

"Heigh-yup!"

The horses' hooves clattered timidly on the drive belt, as though they'd forgotten how to do the work humans needed them to do.

"Heigh-yup!"

The sled jerked, and the runners squeaked.

"Heigh-yup!" the doctor shouted, laughing.

The sled took off.

"Now that's more like it! And not a wolf in sight!" The doctor poked Crouper in the ribs.

"They got 'customed." Crouper smiled with his swollen lip.

They slid smoothly across the field. The snowy road could be seen quite well: it protruded slightly, stretching like a ribbon toward the dark horizon.

"That's more like it. And not a wolf in sight!" the doctor repeated, patting himself on the knees.

He was in a good mood.

The horses slowly gathered speed.

"There we go, there we go . . ." The doctor kept patting his knees happily.

They passed through a bit of forest and came out into a large, clear field again. The moon shone bright.

"Why are they so weak?" the doctor asked, elbowing Crouper. "Don't you feed them well?"

"I feed 'em enough, yur 'onor."

"Give them a taste of the lash, make them run like the wind!"

"They ain't got over their fright as yet."

"What are they—foals?"

"Naw, they ain't foals no more."

"Then why are they so slow? Come now, use the lash!"

"Heigh-yup, c'mon!" Crouper slapped the reins.

The horses sped up a bit. But it wasn't enough for the doctor.

"Why are they crawling along like slugs?! Heigh! Get going!" he said, knocking on the top of the hood.

The horses sped up some more.

"Now that's more like it . . . ," said the doctor happily. "Not much farther to go now. Yup yup! Get going!"

"Heigh-yup, yup!" Crouper shouted and clucked.

He suddenly wanted to show off his horses, although he realized that they were tired.

"Aw, let 'em run for it at the end, maybe as they'll warm 'emselves!" he thought. He himself felt a jolly warmth throughout after polishing off the alcohol.

"Come on now—give them a taste of the whip!" the doctor demanded. "Why are they hiding in there like mice in a pantry? Take that sackcloth off!"

"Well, that's right now, it c'n come off . . . Ain't snowin', and it ain't too cold . . . ," Crouper thought, and deftly unfastened the matting as they went, rolling it up.

The doctor saw the horses' moonlit backs. They looked just like toys.

"Come on, let me . . ." The doctor pulled the whip out of the case.

"Aw, why not let 'im crack it," Crouper thought.

The doctor stood, drew back, and cracked the whip over the horses' backs. "Yip-yip!"

They ran faster. The doctor cracked the whip again:

"Heigh-yuuup!"

The horses snorted and picked up speed. Their legs gleamed and their backs undulated, reminding the doctor of the rough, surging sea that he and Nadine had seen in October in Yalta, the sea he hadn't wanted to enter at all at the time; he'd stood on the shore, staring at the waves, and Nadine, in her striped bathing suit, kept pulling him into the water, teasing him for being overly cautious.

"Heigh-yup!" He lashed the horses so hard that a shiver went down their spines.

They rushed ahead. The sled flew across the field.

"See, that's the way to do it!" the doctor shouted in Crouper's ear.

The frosty air slapped them in the face. Crouper whistled.

The horses ran, and the snow swooshed under the runners.

"That's the ticket! There you go!" The doctor plopped down on the seat, waving the whip. "That's the way to go!"

Crouper whistled as he drove along skillfully. He felt good, too; he realized that it was only another three versts to Dolgoye. The field ended, and fir trees began to appear along the sides of the road. Pretty fir trees, cleared of snow, lined the way.

"Let's goooo!" the doctor shouted, whirling the whip over the horses and knocking the pince-nez off of his nose.

The sled sped through the fir trees. Crouper could make out the contours of a firmly packed bump or hill ahead on the road, but he didn't slow the horses:

"We'll skip on by!"

The sled flew up and hit the hill hard; a crack resounded. The travelers flew off their seats and landed in the snow. The sled stopped on the hill, leaning heavily to one side. The horses snorted and stomped under the hood.

"Damn it . . . ," the doctor muttered. He'd lost his hat, and grabbed his knee, wincing with pain.

"Shit . . ." Crouper pulled his head out of a snowdrift and rubbed the snow off his face.

He floundered about in the drift, looking for his hat, but, on hearing the horses' frightened snorts, he hurried to them and checked under the hood. The horses whickered, looking for help from their master.

"Now, now . . ." Pulling off his mittens, he began petting them gently. "It's all right, all right . . . Not hurt, are ye?"

None of the horses appeared to be injured. The collars and the strong straps had held them.

"Y'er all right, all right . . . Coulda been worse . . ." He stroked their backs, which were damp and steaming from running.

Holding his knee, the doctor moaned. He had whacked it hard against the sled.

Once the horses were calm, Crouper went looking for his hat. Fortunately, the moon was bright and still free of clouds. Crouper soon found the hat, shook the snow off, and stuck it on his head. Then he went over to the doctor. The doctor was sitting in the snow, moaning, shaking his uncovered head, and cursing. Crouper picked up the doctor's hat and put it on him.

"Ain't broke nothing, did ye?" Crouper asked.

"Damn . . ." The doctor felt his knee. "I don't think so. Damn . . . It hurts . . ."

Crouper grabbed him under the arms. Cautiously, the doctor tried to stand but immediately moaned and fell back in the snow:

'Wait a minute . . ."

Crouper squatted nearby and only then realized that he'd broken his lower front tooth against the rudder.

"Ay, darn it . . ." He touched the broken tooth in his mouth, shook his head, and grinned: "How d'ye like that!"

The doctor scooped up snow and held it to his knee:

"Just a minute . . ."

Holding the snow, he turned unseeing eyes on Crouper:

"What was it?"

"Cain't say, yur 'onor . . ." Crouper touched his tooth. "We'll take a look."

"Why didn't you hold the horses back?"

"You was the one floggin' 'em on!"

"I was flogging!" The doctor shook his head indignantly. "I flogged, but you were steering, you damned idiot . . . Damn . . . Hmmm . . . Ouch!"

He winced, leaning over his knee, his fat lips puffing.

"I thought: it's just a little bump, we'll skip right over."

"We sure skipped over it!" the doctor laughed bitterly. "I almost broke my neck . . ."

"And the bump is smooth," said Crouper, standing up and walking over to the sled.

He walked around to the front, looked closely, and froze. He crossed himself:

"God a'mighty. Yur 'onor, take a look at what we runned into."

"Wait, you fool . . . ," the doctor moaned.

"Lord a'mighty, tarnation! Yur 'onor!"

"Shut up, you fool."

"It's a . . . Ain't no one'll believe it . . ."

"Ow . . ." The doctor rubbed his knee. "Give me your hand."

"Lordy, why such a misfortune, what did I do . . . ?" Crouper sat down and anxiously slapped his mittens on his felt boots.

"I said, give me a hand!"

Crouper returned to the doctor and helped him stand:

"God must be mad at me, yur 'onor. Looky what's come 'bout."

He appeared totally lost, and the smile on his birdlike mouth was pitiful, like a beggar's.

The doctor finally managed to stand and straighten up. Leaning on Crouper, he stepped on the hurt leg. He moaned. He stood a bit, panting. He took another step:

"Ow, damn it . . ."

He stood, frowning. Then he hit Crouper upside the head.

"Where have you taken me, you idiot?!"

Crouper didn't even flinch.

"Where've you taken me?!" the doctor screamed into his hat.

A strong, pleasant smell of alcohol came from the doctor.

"Yur 'onor, there's a . . . over there . . ." Crouper shook his head. "Prob'ly better ye don't look."

"You idiot!" The doctor put on his pince-nez, took a step, frowning, glanced at the listing sled, and threw up his hands. "What kind of bastard are you?!"

Crouper said nothing.

"Bastard!"

The doctor's voice thundered through the snow-covered fir trees.

Crouper stepped away toward the tip of the sled and stood there, sniffling.

"Were you just born an idiot or what?" Limping, the doctor hobbled over to him, stopped, and looked.

And froze, his eyebrows raised.

Right in front of the sled, something was sticking out from under the snow. At first the doctor thought it was the twisted stump of an old tree. But when he looked closer, he could make out the head of a dead giant. The sled's right runner had run straight into his left nostril.

The doctor couldn't believe his eyes; he blinked and moved closer: the hill they'd flown up was nothing other than the corpse of one of the *big ones*, covered in snow.

Forgetting all about the pain in his knee, Platon Ilich approached the sled and leaned over. The huge, frozen head had tangled hair, a wrinkled brow, and thick eyebrows; the force of the blow had knocked some of the snow off of it. The runner had disappeared into the nostril of the fleshy nose. The snowflakes on the giant's eyebrows, eyelashes, and hair shimmered silver in the moonlight. One dead eye was full of snow; the other, half closed, stared threateningly at the night sky.

"Oh my God in heaven," muttered the doctor.

"Well, that's the thing of it . . . ," Crouper said with a doomed nod.

The doctor squatted next to the head and brushed the snow off the covered eye. It, too, was half closed. The mouth was hidden in a snowy beard, and the tip of the sled hung above it. Attached to the giant's protruding ear was a heavy copper earring in the form and size of a sixty-pound weight. It sparkled in the snow.

The doctor touched the earring cautiously. He touched the enormous, frozen nose with its rough, greasy, pimply skin. He turned around. Crouper stood there, and from the sorrowful expression on his face one might have thought that the sled had driven into the nostril of his long-lost brother.

The doctor began laughing and fell back into the snow. His laughter rang out amid the firs. The horses replied with uneasy whinnies from inside the sled. This elicited a new fit of laughter from the doctor. He writhed on his back in the snow, laughing, his pince-nez sparkling and his fleshy mouth open wide.

Crouper stood still, like a wet jackdaw. Then he began to cluck his tongue. He smiled and shook his absurdly large hat.

"You're a real master, Kozma!" The doctor wiped the tears of laughter from his eyes.

"Well now, how on earth? . . . No one'd believe it, if'n we told 'em, yur 'onor."

"They certainly wouldn't!" exclaimed the doctor, shaking his hat.

He stood up and brushed off the snow. Limping, he stepped back and looked:

"That lug must be about six meters tall . . . Had to go and kick the bucket here . . ."

Crouper noticed a large, round object under the snow next to the giant's corpse. He pushed the object with his foot, knocking the snow off. A basket of woven twigs appeared. Crouper brushed off the snow with his mitten: glass sparkled. He cleaned the snow off the object. It turned out to be a large, three-bucket, green glass bottle set in a basket holder.

"So that's it, yur 'onor . . ." Crouper cleared the snow from the enormous bottleneck, and sniffed it. "Vodka!"

He kicked the crust of ice on the bottle, knocked it off, and turned it over. Not a drop came out.

"Drunk up the whole thing, he did," Crouper concluded reproachfully.

"He drank it," the doctor agreed, "and gave up the ghost right on the road. There you have it, good old Russian stupidity."

"Coulda least leaned up against a tree," said Crouper, scratching his rear end. He realized he'd said something silly: this giant could only have leaned against a hundred-year-old fir, not one of the young saplings all around.

"Get drunk and collapse on the road . . . Utter idiocy! Russian stupidity!" The red-faced doctor smiled wryly; he took out his cigarette case and lit up the last *papirosa*.

"The worst part is—it's the same runner crashed again, yur 'onor." Crouper sniffed and scratched himself. "If only it hadn't of . . ."

"What?" The doctor didn't follow. He puffed on his cigarette.

"It's the same runner what cracked back apiece."

"You're kidding! The same one? Damn it! So what are you standing around for?! Pull it out of that lout!"

"Just a minute, yur 'onor . . ."

Crouper looked in at the horses, leaned hard against the sled, and clucked:

"C'mon, c'mon, c'mon!"

Snorting, the horses began to step backward. But the sled didn't budge. Crouper realized what the problem was; he looked under the sled and clucked sorrowfully:

"We're just hanging in air, yur 'onor. The drive belt ain't even touchin' the snow."

"Come on, then . . ." Reeking of alcohol and having forgotten about his knee, the doctor clenched the cigarette in his teeth and put his shoulder to the sled. "Come on, nooowww!"

Crouper leaned in, too. The sled shook, but the giant's head didn't release the runner.

"Stuck . . . ," Crouper exhaled.

"Right in the nose!" the doctor exclaimed, and laughed again.

"Have to chop it off." Crouper reached into the coachman's seat for the axe.

"The runner?!" The doctor raised an indignant eyebrow.

"The nose."

"Chop away, my man, chop away." The doctor took one last drag and tossed his cigarette butt aside.

The moon shone brightly. The fir trees stood around like part of a *living* Christmas card.

The doctor unfastened his coat; he was hot. Crouper approached the head, holding the axe in hand. He eyed the head and began to chop at the nostril that the runner had entered. Panting heavily, the doctor leaned his elbow against the sled and watched Crouper's work.

Pieces of frozen flesh flew out from under the axe. Then came a dull thud as the axe struck bone.

"Just don't chop up the runner," the doctor commanded.

"A'course not . . . ," Crouper muttered.

As he hacked away at the enormous frozen nose, Kozma remembered the first time he'd ever seen one of the big people. He was ten at the time. He wasn't living in Dolbeshino but in his father's home in the prosperous village of Pokrovskoye. That summer the autumn fair was moved from Dolgoye to Pokrovskoye. The local merchants decided to cut down Rotten Grove and build stands for the fair. The ancient oak grove had been in Pokrovskoye since the olden days, when there was a landowner's estate house, which had been burned down during the Red Troubles. The oaks in the grove were enormous, dried out, and some of them were decaying and rotting. Boys played war or werewolves in the huge hollows of these oaks. And now they'd decided to cut the grove down. The merchants of Pokrovskoye had hired three giants for this: Avdot, Borka, and Viakhir. On a warm summer evening, they entered Pokrovskoye, each carrying a knapsack, a saw, and a cleaver on his shoulders. Like the frozen creature on the road, these giants were five to six meters tall. Boys greeted them with hoots and whistles. But the big ones treated the little boys like sparrows and paid them no mind. They set up in the old threshing barn of the merchant Baksheev, and in the morning began clearing the oaks. Little Kozma was both frightened and excited as he watched them work: when the big ones went about their task, everything cracked and collapsed. They not only toppled all the oaks, sawed them into logs, and chopped them into pieces, but also pulled the huge oak stumps out by the roots and split them into firewood. In the evenings, they drank about three buckets of milk apiece and ate mashed potatoes with lard; they sat on oak stumps and sang in rough, thundering voices. Kozma remembered one song, which lop-eared, redfaced Avdot had sung in a slow, deep, scary voice:

You carried me, Mátushka,
In your womb,
You wailed, Kasátushka,
Over my tomb.

Then Avdot and Viakhir fought over money. Viakhir beat
Avdot, who got mad and left Pokrovskoye without waiting until
the work was finished. As the womenfolk told it, he spit blood
all along the road from Pokrovskoye to Borovki. Since Avdot left,
the Pokrovskoye merchants paid the giants a third less. So they
had their revenge the last night and took a dump in merchant
Baksheev's well. It took him three days to clean his well after
that; they hauled out buckets and buckets of giant shit . . .

Crouper had trouble chopping through the nose cartilage.
The runner that had caught in the nostril was visible now. Crouper
and the doctor rocked the sled, but the runner wouldn't come
loose.

"The runner pierced the maxillary sinus and got stuck there,"
said the doctor, examining the situation. "Chop right here, from
the top!"

Crouper tore off his mittens, spit on his hands, and began to
chop at the frontal bone. The bone proved hard and thick. Crouper
rested twice as he chopped deeper into it. Pieces of white bone
flew out from under the axe, sparkling in the moonlight.

"When you fell trees, chips will fly," said the doctor, remembering his great-grandfather's favorite saying.

Garin's great-grandfather, an accountant, often reminisced
about the distant Stalin era, when that saying was popular with
the authorities and the people.

Crouper made it through the bone and then, instead of white
chips, greenish ones flew from under the axe.

"Aha! He had sinusitis . . . ," thought the doctor, squinting at the giant professionally. "Probably a vagrant. He was walking, drinking. Got drunk, stumbled, fell asleep. Froze . . .

"Russia . . . ," he muttered, and recalled how he'd once treated a giant who'd developed a hernia. The big one had been hired in Repishnaya for earthwork. He'd dug a foundation pit with his huge shovel, and then moved a barn and overexerted himself. When Garin, along with three volunteers, fixed the hernia, the big one howled, chomped on the chains that had been used to hold him fast to the floor, and roared:

"Don't! Don't!"

They fixed the hernia successfully that time . . .

"Chopped right through, tarnation." Exhausted, Crouper straightened up, took off his hat, and wiped his face.

"Hmm . . ." A cloud had crossed the moon, and in the dim light the doctor examined the light stripe of the runner in the pit of the head. The giant's face, disfigured by the axe, looked ominous.

"Shud we push it back?" Throwing down the axe, Crouper leaned against the nose of the sled.

"Let's push!" The doctor leaned against the other side.

Crouper clicked, clucked, and cooed; the horses began stepping backward, and the runner slid out.

"Thank God!" the doctor sighed in relief.

Crouper dropped to his knees and felt the runner:

"Ay, damnation . . ."

"What is it?" The doctor leaned over and, as the moonlight returned, he could clearly see the broken runner, the point of which had remained forever in the maxillary sinus of the corpse. "Damn . . ."

"Broke off, that's what it did." Panting, Crouper blew his nose loudly.

The doctor instantly felt a chill.

"And what will we do now?" he asked with growing irritation.

Crouper said nothing, he just stood there breathing hard and sniffing. Then he picked up the axe:

"Gots to cut a runner and fix it to this one."

"What, we won't make it?"

"Won't make it this aways."

"We won't make it on the second runner?"

"No, yur 'onor."

"Why not?"

"The other one'll get stuck in the snow—and that'll be the end of it."

The doctor understood.

"It broked off on account of it was cracked already." Crouper sighed. "If it'd been in one piece it wouldn't of broked off. But it was gonna break for sure."

The doctor spat angrily, reached for his cigarettes, and remembered that they were all gone. He spat again.

"Alrighty, I'll go look fer a crooked tree branch," said Crouper, and headed off across the snow into the fir trees.

"Don't be long!" the doctor demanded irritably.

"Depends on how it goes . . ."

He disappeared into the trees.

"Idiot," muttered the doctor after him.

He stood near the ill-starred head awhile, then climbed onto the sled seat, wrapped himself in the rug, pulled his hat down all the way to his eyes, thrust his hands deep in his pockets, and sat motionless. The doctor could still feel the effect of the liquor, but it was beginning to pass, and he felt chilled.

"How absurd!" he thought.

And he quickly dozed off.

He began dreaming of a huge feast in an enormous, brightly lit hall, something like the banquet hall at the House of Scientists in Moscow. It was filled with acquaintances and strangers who had something to do with him, his profession, and his private life; people were congratulating him. They were happy for him, lifted their glasses high for toasts, spoke solemn grandiloquent words, and he, understanding neither the reason for this feast nor the meaning of the congratulations and excitement, forced himself to nod and respond to the congratulations, attempted to carry himself grandly with an air of certainty and joy, although he recognized the problematic nature of the whole affair. Suddenly one of the guests clambered onto the table, and everyone stopped and stared at him. Platon Ilich recognized the man as Professor Amlinsky, who had lectured on suppurative surgery in medical school. Amlinsky, wearing a tuxedo and an attentively tired expression on his beardless face, stood up straight, crossed his hands on his chest theatrically, and without a word began to dance a strange dance, striking the heels of his laced boots hard on the table; there was something ceremonial, sinister, and significant in the dance, which everyone there understood, and which Platon Ilich immediately guessed. He realized that the dance was called "Rogud" and that it was a commemorative *medical* dance, dedicated personally to him, Doctor Platon Ilich Garin, and that all these people gathered at the table had come to Garin's wake. Terror seized Platon Ilich. In a trance, he watched Amlinsky dance with abandon, marking an ominous beat on the table with such force that the dishes jumped and clinked; he danced, making strange circular movements with his rear end and head, first crouching, then straightening up, nodding and winking at everyone. The miller's wife sat near Platon Ilich. She was beautifully dressed; a spray of diamonds shone around her plump, well-groomed face. She was Amlinsky's wife, and had been for a long time, as it happened. The air was fragrant with perfume and the smells of her smooth, well-tended body. Her vivid face drew close to Garin's, and she whispered to him with a lewd smile:

"A meaty, pompous hint!"

The doctor woke up.

As soon as he moved, a ferocious shudder shook his body. Trembling, he lifted the hat from his eyes. It was dark and cold all around. Crouper was chopping something in the darkness. The moon had hidden behind clouds.

The doctor moved some more, but the shivers went through him so profoundly that he bellowed, and his teeth began to chatter. He was suddenly frightened. He had never experienced such terrifying, penetrating cold in his life. He realized that he would never get out of this accursed, endless winter night

"L-lor-d-d h li-have m m-mer-cy . . . ," he began to pray, his teeth chattering so hard and fast it was as though someone had attached them to a motor made by the Klacker company.

Crouper continued to chop in the darkness.

"Lo-lo-lor-d-d . . . p-pro-t-tec-t m-me and lead-d m-me . . . ," the doctor moaned, trembling, as though in pain.

"There now . . . ," he heard Crouper mutter, and the chopping stopped.

While the doctor dozed, Crouper had found a small fir tree with a bent trunk in the forest; he had cut it down, chopped off the branches, attached it to the sled, and whittled it into a semblance of a runner. It wasn't much to look at, was even ridiculous looking, but was quite capable of getting them to Dolgoye. It had to be nailed to the broken runner. And there was even the means: when Crouper had repaired the runner at the miller's, he'd grabbed three nails.

"Shuda taken at least four," he thought.

But he reassured himself aloud: "Three'll do it."

Noticing that the doctor was agitated and mumbling, Crouper went up to him:

"Yur 'onor, help me out."

"L-lord . . . Lor-d-d . . ." The doctor shook.

"Cold?" Crouper realized.

After working, he wasn't cold.

"St-st-start a f-fire . . . ," the doctor chattered.

"A fire?" Crouper scratched under his hat and looked up at the hidden moon. "That's right, now . . . Cain't see a darn thing . . . Won't hit the nail . . ."

"St-st-start . . . st-st-st-start . . ." The doctor kept shaking as though he were feverish.

"Just give me a minute."

Grabbing the axe, Crouper went into the fir grove to look for a dry tree. He had to look for some time: as if to thwart him, the moon stayed behind clouds, and he had to feel about. The dry fir turned out to be larger than the others, and its hard, withered trunk wouldn't take the axe blade. Crouper hacked for a long time. When he'd cut it down, he dragged it toward the sled but got stuck between two other fir trees and fussed about, chopping off branches in the darkness, almost whacking himself in the leg in the process.

Panting, he dragged the tree to the sled.

The doctor was still sitting on his seat, bent over, with his hands in his pockets.

"Oy, the doctor's gone and froze plain through . . . ," thought Crouper. Taking a deep breath, he began to chop branches off the tree.

When he had a fair number, he gathered bunches of thin twigs, broke them in half, took out a lighter, and aimed the blue stream of gas. The fire caught quickly. Crouper dug out the snow with his boot, stuck the burning twigs in the hole, and piled on more branches.

Soon the fire was blazing.

"Doctor, come, get warm!" Crouper shouted.

The doctor pried open his eyelids: tongues of flame danced in the reflection of his pince-nez. He began the painful process of standing up. He had to move his stiff, shivering body to the fire. He shook; from sitting so long, his legs wouldn't obey him. He moved like a zombie just arisen from the dead. Approaching the fire, he walked straight into the flames, like a drunken fireman.

"Where ye goin'? You'll burn up!" exclaimed Crouper, pushing him away.

The doctor sat down on the snow and crawled to the fire; he thrust his gloved hands into it.

"Well, go on and burn, then, if you wanna," Crouper muttered, breaking off a branch.

Soon the doctor cried out and jerked his hands out of the fire; his gloves were smoking.

"Open up yur coat, yur 'onor, so the heat c'n get inside," Crouper recommended.

Squinting from the smoke, the doctor unfastened his coat with shaking hands.

"There ye go." Crouper smiled tiredly.

His face was haggard, but his birdlike smile hadn't dimmed.

They warmed themselves until they'd burned the whole tree. The doctor came round and had stopped shaking. But he was still frightened.

"Why am I afraid?" he thought, gazing at the scattering of small orange embers from the twigs. "It's dark. It's cold. So what? Dolgoye is nearby . . . He's not scared. And I shouldn't . . ."

"Yur 'onor, help me out with the runner?" Crouper asked, picking up the axe from the melting snow.

"What?" The doctor didn't understand.

"I cut a tip. You hold it, and I'll nail it. I got three nails."

The doctor rose silently and fastened his coat. Crouper lit the last fir branch and stuck it in the snow next to the giant's head. Fire shone in the corpse's frozen eyes, and the doctor noticed that they were green.

"Let's go, while it's still burning!" Crouper ordered, falling to his knees and placing the tip under the broken runner.

The doctor also kneeled, grabbed the pieces of wood, and held them together. Crouper took the three precious nails out of his pocket, put two of them between his teeth, set one in place, and pounded it with three strikes of the axe head. He placed the second nail and knocked it in just as skillfully, but on the fourth strike the axe missed and hit his left hand hard. "Darn!" he exclaimed, and the third nail fell out of his mouth.

The branch burned out, scattering amber ashes.

"Ay . . ." Shaking his large hand, Crouper dropped the axe and fumbled in the snow. "Where d'ye go . . ."

The doctor felt about in the snow, too. But they couldn't find the nail.

"You need light," the doctor ordered.

"Hold on now . . ." Crouper felt around, collected the remaining twigs, and lit them.

But the brief flame didn't help: the nail appeared to have melted into the snow.

"What a fix . . . ," Crouper said sorrowfully, crawling about the snow.

"What the . . . How'd you . . . ," the doctor mumbled, groping around.

"An idiot, that's how come I dropped it," Crouper explained.

They searched a bit longer in the faint, bluish light of two lighters, but didn't find the nail.

"All my fault . . ." Covered in snow, Crouper kept looking around the runner.

He was very upset about losing the nail. He began to regret that he'd taken only three, out of stupidity and timidity—that he'd been afraid to take at least four nails from the tin.

"Idiot. I'm an idiot."

He blew his nose, and then used the axe to bend the end of the two nails, which had come out the underside of the freshly hewn boards. He touched them:

"Will we make it on two nails?"

"Strap it with a bandage." Leaning over, the doctor stared at the repaired runner.

"We c'n do that," Crouper nodded indifferently. He stood up and opened the hood.

The horses whinnied. Crouper could feel that they were cold.

"C'mon, c'mon, talk to me . . ." Pulling off his mittens, he started petting and stroking them.

Faint neighs came from under the hood along with steam from the horses. Heated by the horses' bodies, the space under the hood was the only warm place. The doctor was jealous, and it irritated him that people were freezing but horses were capable of warming themselves. He found the remainder of the bandages, and they wrapped the ill-fated runner. The doctor had hardly finished tying his traditional knot when he heard a faint noise at his back. He lifted his head: it was snowing.

"Damn it!" he exclaimed, looking at the sky.

The sky was thick with clouds. There was no longer any bright moon, nor any sparkling splatter of stars. Snow fell straight down in heaps; it was falling so thickly that everything around disappeared. As though mocking the travelers, taking revenge for an hour or so of brightness and calm, the snow fell heavy, fast, and dense.

"Just what we was waitin' fer . . ." Crouper grinned wryly and covered the horses.

"How will we go on?" the doctor asked, looking around.

"We'll just go on, like God wills," Crouper answered. He moved the rudder to the left and shouted at the horses.

The sled jerked, and slid off the corpse. Crouper directed it onto what should have been the road, and walked alongside it. The doctor followed.

"Have a seat, yur 'onor. I'll walk!" Crouper shouted.

The doctor climbed onto the seat.

"How much farther is it?"

"I dunno. 'Bout three versts . . ."

"We have to get there!"

"We'll get there, God willing . . ."

"Three versts. You can walk that far?"

"Yep . . ."

The doctor desperately wanted to get out of this snowy eternity, out of the cold, which hadn't abandoned him for a moment, out of the night, which was like a bad dream; he wanted to forget all of it forever, along with the snow, this ridiculous sled, this cretin Crouper, and the broken runner.

"Lord, lead me, protect and guide me . . . ," he prayed to himself, and counted every meter of road as it passed.

Crouper walked along, steering, raking through the snow with his felt boots, sinking into it, and getting up again. Ahead and all around them was a wall of silently falling snow. The silence and total absence of wind scared the doctor even more.

Crouper wasn't scared. He was simply tired of it all, so tired that he was on his last legs, trying not to collapse and fall asleep. The fire had sapped his strength, he'd inhaled a lot of smoke, and now he wanted but one thing—to sleep.

"Three versts . . . We'll get there if'n we don't lose the road . . . ," he thought, fighting to keep his eyes open as they stuck together from the snow and exhaustion.

About half a verst on, when the fir forest ended and a clear field began, they strayed off track. Crouper wandered around and found the road. They set off but lost the road again. And, again, Crouper found the road. The doctor no longer bothered to get off the sled; he just sat, covered with snow, praying and stiffening with fear. They rode on successfully for another half a verst, but suddenly there was a crack, and the sled listed treacherously to the right: they had run off the road into a gully, and the repaired runner broke.

"It broke off!" Crouper shouted, as he fussed about in the snow.

"Just you . . ." The doctor had been motionless the whole way, but he suddenly jumped down from his seat; up to his knees in snow, he hurried to the trunk and began furiously unfastening his travel bags.

"Go to hell, you idiot . . . Go to hell with your sled . . . and your stinking runner . . ." He untied the snow-covered travel bags, grabbed them, and walked off.

Crouper didn't stop him. He no longer had the strength to stand, so he slumped down next to the sled, leaning his back against it; he held onto the broken runner as though it were a broken leg.

"I could have walked there faster!" the doctor shouted without turning around.

He strode ahead along the snowy road.

"Listening to idiots and assholes my whole life!" he muttered angrily to himself as he moved along through the thick snowfall and darkness. "Listening to idiots! And assholes! What kind of life is that?! My God, what kind of life is that?!"

His indignation energized him as he moved through the whooshing snow, his boots stirring up an endless white porridge. He could feel the road with his feet, the well-traveled crust of ice covered with fresh snow.

"Straight on, just keep going straight on . . . ," thought the doctor, keeping up his pace.

He realized that he shouldn't fear this lifeless, cold element, but should simply keep moving and moving, overcoming it.

The snowy dark enveloped Dr. Garin. He walked and walked. The sled, Crouper, the little horses—all that was behind him, like a disappointing past; ahead was the road that he had to travel.

"Dolgoye is close . . . I should have left that fool and walked . . . I would have reached it long ago . . ."

He took a step, sank into a ditch, and fell, losing his travel bags. Floundering in the snow, he found the bags, clambered out of the ditch and went back a bit, barely able to make out his tracks in the darkness. He found the road and kept to the right, but again he fell into a ditch, deeper than the first one.

"A ravine . . . ," he thought.

Apparently, the road passed through a ravine.

"A bend in the road," thought the panting doctor.

He climbed out of the ditch, took a few steps, and sank into the snow again. There were gullies on all sides.

"Where is the road?" He straightened his hat, which had slipped down over his eyes.

He began to feel carefully for the road with his foot, trying not to sink into the snow. There was something uneven under the snow, and it didn't feel at all like a road. The road seemed to dissolve into gullies. Searching for the road, the doctor lost all strength and sat down on the snow. His legs grew cold.

"Damnation . . . ," he muttered.

He sat awhile, then stood up and grabbed his travel bags. He decided to go straight through the damned ravines, in the hope of coming out onto the road. This turned out to be a difficult proposition: he walked, falling and getting up, sinking into the snow and climbing out. But he couldn't find the road. It was as though ravines had devoured it.

Utterly exhausted, he sat down. The snow, the endless snow, kept falling in heaps from the dark sky, covering the doctor and his tracks.

The doctor started to doze off, and he shivered.

"Just don't fall asleep . . . ," he muttered. He stood up and, barely moving, walked on.

There was no end to the gullies. Sinking into the snow yet another time, he lay on his side and crawled ahead, pulling his heavy bags after him.

Suddenly, he felt something even and hard underfoot.

"Here it is!" he exclaimed hoarsely.

Climbing out of the ravine onto the road, he stood a moment, breathing heavily; he set the bags down and crossed himself: "Thank the Lord."

He picked up his travel bags and walked on ahead. He hadn't gone more than twenty steps when something moved toward him out of the snowy darkness and appeared to hang right overhead. Staring with wide-open eyes, the doctor could make out something like the trunk of a bent tree overhead, plastered in snow. He began to go around from the left when suddenly he noticed something behind the trunk, something huge and wide that occupied the entire road and from which this trunk extended. The doctor approached cautiously. The huge, wide object was completely covered in snow and rose up and up. Throwing his travel bags down in the snow, the doctor wiped his pince-nez with his scarf and tilted his head back. He couldn't understand what was in front of him. At first he thought it was a pointed haystack covered in snow. But he touched it and realized that it wasn't made of hay, just snow. His eyes agog, the doctor stepped farther back. Suddenly, at the top of the strange, vast, snowy shape, he made out the likeness of a human face. He realized that he was standing in front of a snowman of monstrous proportions, with a huge, erect phallus of snow.

"Lord Almighty . . . ," the doctor mumbled, and crossed himself.

The snowman was the height of a two-story building. Its phallus hung threateningly over Dr. Garin's head. The snowman looked out of the darkness through two round cobblestone eyes pressed into the snow by a powerful, unknown sculptor. An aspen root protruded in place of a nose.

"God Almighty . . . ," the doctor muttered, and took off his hat.

He felt hot. He remembered the giant's corpse and realized

that the big one, into whose nose the sled had driven not long ago, was the sculptor of this snow monster. Before his drunken death, he had decided to make something for indifferent and distant humanity from the materials on hand.

The doctor reached up and swung his hat, trying to reach the white phallus above. But he couldn't. The huge pole hung over him, aimed ominously at the darkness. Snow whirled about, falling on the phallus and on Garin's uncovered head. The doctor realized that the giant had stuck a tree trunk in the snowman's belly and packed snow around it. The result resembled an aroused male reproductive organ. The blizzard snowfall had made it even thicker.

Garin took a few steps back to look at the snow giant. It stood with a sort of unflinching readiness to pierce the surrounding world with its phallus. The doctor met the gaze of the cobblestone eyes. The snowman looked at Garin. The hair on the doctor's head tingled. Terror seized him.

He screamed and ran away.

He ran, stumbled, fell, got up, and, moaning with fear, ran and kept on running.

Finally, he ran into something at chest level and fell flat on his back. It was a forceful blow; it knocked the breath out of him, and colored lights swam before his eyes. He groaned in pain. He gradually caught his breath. He was cold; he looked around and saw that his right hand was holding his hat. He sat up and pulled the hat on his head.

He shivered. Shaking and holding his injured chest, he stood up. In front of him, sticking out of the snow like a milepost, was the broken trunk from an old birch tree. The doctor held on to it, afraid of collapsing in the snow. He pressed against the birch and stood still, breathing heavily. The birch was old, and the bark was puckered. Holding on to the birch, the doctor breathed on it and inhaled its fragrance. The frozen birch smelled like the bathhouse.

"White . . . cellulose . . . ," the doctor mumbled into the silver bark.

He realized that he was beginning to freeze.

"Move, move . . ." He pushed away from the birch and walked on through the falling snow.

He walked without feeling the road, walked through the deep snow, tripped, fell, got up again, and walked on and on and on. In front of him, to the side, and behind him it was all the same—the darkness of night, and falling snow. The doctor kept on walking.

Soon he began to move more slowly, and had more trouble getting out of ditches; he staggered and lost his balance. The snow wouldn't let go of him, it clutched at his stiffened, disobedient legs. The doctor moved slower and slower. His fingers were freezing; he thrust his wet gloves deep into his pockets and walked on, hunched over.

His knees began to give way. He kept going, but could barely drag his legs forward.

Just when he was about to fall and remain forever stuck in the endless snow, something stopped him. Brushing the snow from his freezing eyelids, the doctor could make out the back of the sled, decorated with roses and notched by an axe along the edges. He couldn't believe his eyes, and reached out to touch it. Standing there, holding on to the back, he caught his breath. He looked over: the seat was empty. There was no one in the sled.

The hair on his head stood up again. He realized that Crouper had left, abandoned the sled, and abandoned the doctor, abandoned him forever, and that now he was completely alone, alone

forever in this winter, in this field, in this snow. And that this—
was death.

"Death . . . ," the doctor said hoarsely, and he felt like crying
out of self-pity.

But he had no tears, nor the strength to cry. He fell to his
knees next to the sled.

He thought he heard the neighing of a little horse somewhere
not far away. But he didn't believe it.

His frozen lips trembled, and something like a sob emerged
from his mouth.

The horse neighed again, quite close by. He looked around.
There was nothing but deadly, relentless dark space. Once again a
horse neighed and snorted. He remembered the voice: it was the
mischievous roan stallion. And he was neighing in the sled. The
doctor stared at it in bewilderment.

Suddenly he noticed that the matting that had always covered the hood was all buckled. Thinking it was snow that had
fallen on top, the doctor touched the matting. It moved. He opened
it a bit.

From inside the dark hood came the smell of horses' warm
breath; inside, the horses tossed their manes, snorted, and neighed.
And Crouper's voice exclaimed:

"Doctor!"

The doctor looked into the hood, stunned. He reached out
his hand and touched it. Crouper lay inside, all curled up with
the horses.

"You . . . How?" The doctor wheezed.

"Crawl in," said Crouper, turning and scooting over. "It's warm
in here. Not long till morning. We'll wait it out."

The doctor wanted desperately to get inside that dark, warm
space, which smelled so sweetly of horses. He clambered under

the hood in an awkward rush. Crouper gathered the horses to-gether, freeing up space for the doctor, who barely managed to squeeze in: his icy chin touched Crouper's warm forehead, while his arms and legs squashed the little horses. They neighed un-easily. Crouper helped them to get out from under Garin:

"Don't be afeard, nothin' to be afeard of . . ."

The hood made a loud cracking sound when the doctor's large body crowded in. Crouper lay on his right side and made as much room as he could, allowing the doctor's wet knees between his legs, pushing the uneasily neighing horses on top of himself and onto the doctor, who lay on his left side. Heaving about like a bear in a den, the doctor wasn't thinking about the horses or Crouper, he just wanted to hide from the accursed cold, to warm himself.

Somehow they settled down. The horses lay on top of them, huddled together between their legs, and Crouper even managed to place some of them against his neck. He finally managed to free his left arm to reach up and pull the overhead matting closed.

It was totally dark inside the hood now.

"Well, there we goes . . . ," Crouper muttered into the doctor's chest, which smelled of sweat and eau de cologne.

Garin was uncomfortable; his hat slipped down over his eyes, but he had no desire to straighten it: he only had enough energy left to breathe. Four horses moved about on his hat. Three others had nested on Crouper's hat.

"I was thinkin' ye wasn't gonna come back nohow," Crouper spoke into the doctor's chest.

The doctor was still breathing heavily. Then he suddenly turned sharply, pressing his knees into Crouper. A loud crack sounded behind Crouper's back: the hood split.

"Ay . . ." Crouper could feel the crack against his back.

The doctor stopped turning.

"I couldn't find the road," he whispered hoarsely.

" 'Course not. It's under snow."

"Under snow."

"Cain't see nothin' out there."

"Not a thing."

They stopped talking. The horses quickly settled down and grew quiet, too. The mischievous roan had thrust his head up his master's sleeve and was nipping him on the arm.

"And . . . uh . . . the . . . um . . ." The doctor tried to ask something.

"Wha?"

"Your horses."

"The horses is here, 'course they is."

"They're . . . keeping warm?"

"They're warmin' us, yur 'onor. And we're warmin' 'em. Together we'll stay warm."

"We'll stay warm?"

"We'll stay warm."

The doctor was silent a moment and then, with barely audible voice:

"I'm frozen. Nearly through."

" 'Course ye are."

"I don't want to die."

"God willin'—ye won't die. It'll be light soon. Then, when we c'n see, we'll fix the runner and set off. Else'n someone passin' by'll hook us up."

"Hook us?"

"Could be. Hook us and tow us in."

"People actually . . . travel along this way?" asked the doctor.

" 'Course they do. The bread men come early mornin', people gotta have bread, don't they? I hitch up at seven. And in your

Dolgoye there, people wants to eat, too. Someone'll tow us—and we'll get to Dolgoye, 'course we will."

Hearing about Dolgoye as he fell into a deep sleep, the doctor had trouble understanding what it was, but then remembered that he, Dr. Garin, was on his way to Dolgoye, that he had to bring the vaccine there, that Zilberstein, who'd given the first vaccine dose, was waiting for him, and that he, Garin, was carrying the second dose of vaccine, which was so important, so crucial for people infected with the *Bolivian plague*. He remembered his travel bags, but then remembered that he had dropped them near that ominous snowman, though maybe he hadn't left them, maybe he picked them up and ran away with them. "Did I leave them or not?" He had trouble remembering. "No, I didn't leave them, no . . . How could I leave them? It would be impossible to leave them . . ." He realized that he'd grabbed them under his arms and run with them, run across the snow, the deep, thick snow, run, run, run, and the snow had stopped, and then it began to melt, melt away, and the grove was flooded with sunlight, the white birch grove, the grove near the church at Nikolaevsky, the one where he and Irina were supposed to be married, she was waiting for him in the church, and he was walking through the grove, through the warm, almost hot, summer grove, the bright grass was bathed in sunlight, bumblebees buzzed about, the birch trunks were warm, heated by the sun, he tucked one of his bags under his arm, and with his free hand touched the hot trunks of the birches with great pleasure; he could already see the church, carriages crowded around it, someone had even come by automobile, it was the banker Gorsky, who else would travel by car? He walked and walked, but suddenly the earth heaved under his feet, and he realized that under the earth, under this loose, warm, summer earth were residents of Dolgoye, infected with *the*

Bolivian Black; they had dug tunnels, he hadn't vaccinated them and they had turned into zombies, they'd gone underground, dug out tunnels, and reached him: they were here, and he ran toward the church, through the grove, ran as fast as he could, but the zombies' hands, their inhuman, clawlike hands that resembled the paws of a mole—it was called the "mole-paw syndrome," *pes talpae*—were coming out of the earth, reaching through the grass, grabbing him by the feet, their claws dug into him painfully, they were strong and sharp, they tore off his new patent-leather shoes, but he escaped the claws and ran to the church, and everyone was inside and the priest already stood at the pulpit, Irina wore her wedding dress and stood holding a candle; he stood next to her, someone handed him a candle, he could feel the floor of the church with the soles of his bare feet, the floor was hot, very hot, the earth under it was hot, heated by the zombies' furious movements, but he liked the feeling, it was so pleasant to feel the heat of the marble floor with his feet that he didn't want to follow the priest, didn't want to circle the pulpit with Irina, no, he felt fine just like this, so fine that tears poured from his eyes, and he stood still, and everyone understood him, everyone shared his joy, everyone felt so good, but he was rapturously happy, because he loved everyone, everyone standing in this church, he loved Irina, he loved the priest, he loved his family and friends, he loved the zombies, too, who were stirring and moaning under the floor of the church, he loved everyone, everyone, and now everyone began to move around him, because he couldn't detach his feet from the *amazing* warmth; all the guests, the priest, the archdeacon with his roaring bass, the singers, and Irina, everyone was circling, circling him, walking and singing, and underground the zombies were circling the church, and they were singing, too, singing into the earth, singing with an earthy buzz, like huge earthen bees, they buzzed underground, they buzzed and droned "many long years . . . ," and their buzz was so loud and sweet that it tickled, and everyone circled round and round Garin, like the earth's axis, and all the buzzing and circling made the doctor and his feet ever warmer and joyful . . .

Crouper felt that the doctor had fallen asleep; he turned slightly and rearranged the horses on him and in empty spaces.

"Everbody's in one piece . . . They fits . . . And me and the doctor fits . . . ," he thought. "Well, that's that."

Everything was fine under the hood: the doctor, Crouper, and the horses all had enough room. Only one thing was worrisome: the crack. The wood had split along the seam, just behind Crouper's back, and as bad luck would have it, his sheepskin coat had an old hole right near the left shoulder—last winter he'd caught it on a latch in the Khliupin bakery when he was carrying out a tray of bread. He'd sewn it up with a coarse thread and gotten through that winter, but now the thread had apparently frayed, and a draft from the crack was blowing right onto his left shoulder blade, and he couldn't turn over because the doctor was asleep.

"Bad luck . . . ," Crouper thought, turning slightly to protect the horses, shifting his left shoulder away from the crack, trying to put his back against it.

One of the horses got its head tangled in his beard.

"Who's that tickling me there?" Crouper grinned.

The horse whinnied.

"Sivka, what is it?" Crouper recognized the voice of one of his four gray geldings.

The gelding whickered on hearing its name. Then it urinated on Crouper's chest.

"Don't get all worked up now." Crouper pushed the horse's head gently with his chin.

The gray drew back and poked his muzzle into Crouper's neck, where two other horses were already nuzzling him. Hearing the gray's voice, the lively roan, who had been about to doze off inside his master's sleeve, grew jealous and neighed aggressively.

"What's got into ye?" Crouper flicked him on the withers, which protruded from his sleeve.

The roan quieted down and nibbled his master's arm with playful gratitude.

"There's my gadfly . . . ," Crouper thought about the roan; smiling in the darkness, he remembered how he had brought him home last summer under his shirt.

Previously, Crouper only had a black roan in the herd. He traded a canister of gasoline to a visiting tailor in Khliupin for the six-month-old red roan colt. He had bought the canister from his brother-in-law, and had already loaded it on the cart of the late land surveyor Romych, when a drunken tailor showed up and began boasting that he'd been paid for two women's dresses and two velour jackets with a little colt. He pulled the roan out of his pocket and showed it to Crouper. The roan's coloring was unusual; he was red with streaks of gray, a fiery mane, and he was vigorous, though not very broad-chested. He neighed continually. Crouper liked him from the start. Perhaps because he'd recently lost two colts to some unknown disease and there were two empty collars in the third row. Or maybe because the roan was a redhead, like Crouper himself. The tailor kept on babbling, saying he would raise the colt and rent it out to coachmen. But when Crouper offered him the canister of 92-grade gasoline, he quickly agreed. On the way home the roan neighed uneasily under Crouper's shirt. Nor did he calm down in the herd. His lively, brash temperament distinguished him from the others, but he wasn't lead material. The lead horse was always the calm bay, a broad-chested gelding.

Crouper twisted around, trying to protect the tear at his shoulder from the gap. Cold rose from the frozen plank floor of the hood. The only warmth came from the horses. Even in the darkness, Crouper could feel where each and every animal was. He knew that the eight chestnuts, who always gathered in their own herd, had managed even now to huddle together in the spaces between the doctor's legs and Crouper's. The doctor was sleeping, breathing hoarsely onto Crouper's forehead. He was a large man, and his arms and legs filled almost the entire space under the hood.

"A big fellow . . . ," Crouper thought, and suddenly remembered the giant's corpse and its hard forehead, which he had hacked to pieces.

"Chopped and chopped, I did . . . and barely managed to chop it open . . . ," he thought, yawning with a shiver.

He shivered every now and then. He hadn't been this tired for ages. The exhaustion of the endless road was so intense that he no longer noticed the cold. He didn't want to move, even though a draft was blowing on his shoulder. The shivering and exhaustion felt sweet, much like when he was a child.

"Thank God it isn't too freezing . . . ," he thought as he dozed off.

Sleep carried him into its own expanses. As he fell asleep, Crouper remembered the cleaver the giants had in Pokrovskoye when he was little. That enormous, massively heavy cleaver didn't look like the ordinary axes the peasants used to split firewood:

there was a hole that ran through the side, with an iron grommet in it that passed through the handle. The men were surprised: in normal cleavers and axes, the cleat wedges were lodged in the butt end of the axe handle, but in this case they were on the side.

That grommet, the grommet from the giants' cleaver, was big. Very big. Heavy. Weighty. It weighed many poods, hundreds, thousands of poods, and stretched, stretched, stretched from merchant Baksheev's house to the house of Crouper's father, a sturdy house with a weathervane, a super-antenna, and pink gingerbread-house-style decorative window frames, the very house that Crouper burned down when he was a little boy, burned down when he and Funtik found some Chinese firecrackers, and his parents and Uncle Misha and his sister Polina were in the fields, and Funtik placed a cartridge of firecrackers on a Three Warriors beer box, and they lit them, and the firecrackers went off, the box fell over for some reason, the cartridge flew in the air and popped in all directions, and the firecrackers landed on the drying barn, the straw roof, and the house, right up top, shooting straight into the open attic, where Father had laid out beeswax on paper; the roof of the drying barn caught fire, the inside of the attic caught fire, and Funtik got scared and ran off, but Kozma, who was also scared, didn't run away and didn't cry out, he just stood there and watched the drying barn burn, he stood and watched, stood and watched, he kept on standing and watching the fire while the roof burned and flames jumped to the hayloft and the hayloft caught fire; he was still standing and watching when the neighbors ran over; the attic room under the roof was blazing, there were flames coming from the window, the house could no longer be saved, and the neighbors were dragging things out; but he, Kozma, was supposed to save something important in the house, something that burned back then but wouldn't burn now, something his father couldn't forgive him for at the time, though he forgave him the burned house, the drying barn, and the hayloft, but for the fact that this thing had burned he could never forgive him, which was why Kozma left his father's house so early, but now he would be able to save the thing, he'd know how to drag it out of the house, he only has to force himself to do it, to move from that spot, and he grabs hold of his leg and lifts it with his hands, he moves it, then grabs the other one and moves it; his legs don't want to walk, but he grabs them, digs into them, tears the flesh with his nails until he bleeds, moves them, moves the flesh of his legs, his hands walk his legs, his hands, his hands make his legs walk; bending over his legs and forcing himself to walk, he enters the house, the house is already hot, the upstairs is burning, burning fast, the neighbors have taken everything out, they've saved the icons and both trunks, but only he knows where the most important thing is hidden, his father's greatest treasure. He grabs the ring of the cellar trapdoor, pulls, lifts the wood trap, and climbs down into the cellar; there are barrels of marinated cabbage and pickles, a ham wrapped in cheesecloth hangs from a beam, and next to the ham, also wrapped in cheesecloth, disguised as meat, hangs the cocoon of a large butterfly, it's the size of a leg of meat, but the wingspan of the butterfly that will hatch from this cocoon is more than two meters, his father and uncle stole it from the royal incubator near Podolsk, his uncle was working in the greenhouses for the season, they took the cocoon out and hid it in a wheelbarrow full of peat, took it to Pokrovskoye, his father hid it in the cellar, disguised as a leg of salted beef, wrapped it in cheesecloth, rubbed it with lard, the cocoon of a huge blue Death's Head; it was very expensive, very beautiful, it cost three times more than Father's house, Father had already arranged to sell it to the Romanians, the main thing was to keep it in a cool place so that the butterfly didn't hatch too early or everything would be ruined. Kozma must take it out of the house and quickly hide it in the old cellar in the garden, where it is also cold, and Father would return, and the cocoon would be safe; he gropes for it in the cellar and holds it in his arms, it's like an infant, he crawls out of the cellar with it, and everything around is burning, everything has caught fire so fast, everything is in flames, it's so hot, so bright, he heads for the door carrying the cocoon, but suddenly it cracks, he keeps going, but it cracks, and a dark-blue, unbelievably beautiful butterfly begins to burst out of the cocoon, bursts out of the membrane, bursts out of his hands, it is so lovely, so smooth, silky, incredibly beautiful, so beautiful that he forgets about his father, it's pretty, like an angel, it has a beautiful, light-blue shining skull on its back, but it isn't really a skull, it's an angelic face, a sublime angelic visage, shining in every tint of blue and violet, it sings in a delicate, quivering voice, and it tears away, tears out of his hands, its huge wings flap, it tears away so forcefully, so charmingly, that Kozma's heart begins to quiver like its wings, he can't let it go, he mustn't let it go, he'll do anything to hold on to it, he grabs it by its thick, silky legs, it sings, flaps its wings, and flies through the burning window, it carries Kozma through the fiery window, and Kozma's arms join with the butterfly's legs, his bones fuse with its bones, his bones sing along with the butterfly, a song of new life, a song of ultimate happiness, a song of great joy; they sing, and the butterfly carries him into the infinite fiery window, into the narrow fiery window, into the swift window of fire, into the long window of fire, into the window of fire, into the window of fire, into the window of fire.

The sun sparkled on the gray horizon. It illuminated the snowy field and the clear pale-blue sky with its fading stars and moon. A ray of sun, stretching across the field, touched the snow-covered sled, hit the crack in the hood and the eye of one of the four horses sleeping on the doctor's fur hat. The dark bay stallion opened one eye.

The crunch of snow could be heard next to the hood. Something outside was scratching at the plywood. The bright red muzzle of a fox poked under the matting. The dark bay neighed in terror. The other horses turned over and woke up. They saw the fox and whinnied, bolting back. The fox grabbed the first horse it could, and took off. The horses neighed and reared.

The neighing rang painfully in the doctor's left ear. He thought that neurosurgeons were drilling into his ear. He just managed to open his eyes. And saw nothing but darkness. The darkness was whickering. The doctor wanted to move his right arm. But he couldn't. He moved the fingers of his left hand. His left hand was under the flap of his fur coat. He pulled the numb, disobedient hand out from under the coat and felt for his face with his stiff, frozen fingers. His hat was on his face. With tremendous difficulty, the doctor managed to move the hat off his face with those disobedient fingers. The ray of sun immediately hit his left eye. The horses neighed, and their hooves trampled the doctor's body and head.

The doctor opened his eyes wide but couldn't see anything and didn't understand where or who he was.

He tried to move. Nothing worked. His body wouldn't obey, as though he weren't even there. He unstuck his lips and sucked freezing air into his lungs. He exhaled it. His breath billowed in the ray of sun. The little horses stomped on the doctor. He made a huge effort to raise his head. His chin ran up against something smooth and cold. The horses jumped off the hat. The doctor moved slightly. Pain shot through his back and shoulders: his entire body had grown numb and stiff with cold.

The doctor's mouth opened, but instead of a moan a weak rasp emerged. He tried to raise himself a tiny bit. But something was hindering his body and legs, which he couldn't feel at all.

The sunlight beat painfully in his eyes. The doctor remembered his pince-nez and patted his chest to find it. But his fingers wouldn't work right, and something cold and strong was preventing him from finding the pince-nez. Finally he located it and pulled it to his face.

Suddenly, he heard loud human voices outside. The matting was torn abruptly from the hood. Two human silhouettes hung over the doctor's head, blocking out the sun.

"*Ni hai huozhe ma?*" one of the silhouettes asked, not sure whether the doctor was still alive.

"*Wo kao!*" The other man laughed.

Frowning, the doctor put the pince-nez to his eyes. Two Chinese men were leaning over him. The horses whinnied and snorted. The doctor tried to turn, holding the pince-nez to his eyes, but the cord of the pince-nez caught on something. It was Crouper's nose. His face was close, and it seemed to the doctor that it filled the entire hood. The huge face was lifeless and wax-white; only the sharp nose was blue. The sun shone on Crouper's frost-covered eyelashes and his icy beard. His pale lips had frozen in a half smile. The expression on his face was now even more birdlike, mockingly self-assured, surprised by nothing and afraid of nothing.

A live hand stretched out, touched Crouper's cold face, and quickly withdrew.

"Gua le!" Then the warm, rough fingers of another hand touched the doctor's cheeks.

"You alive?" a voice asked in Russian.

The doctor suddenly remembered everything.

"Who are you?" the voice asked him.

He opened his mouth to answer, but instead of words only a raspy noise and steam came out.

"Wo shi yisheng," the doctor croaked in horrible Chinese. *"Bangzhu . . . bangzhu . . . qing ban wo . . . "*

"You're a doctor? Don't worry, we'll help you."

"Wo yisheng, wo shi yisheng . . . ," Platon Ilich rasped, his hand with the pince-nez trembling.

The older Chinese began speaking Mandarin on his cell phone: "Shen, get a bag of some kind over here, there's a bunch of little horses, and bring Ma, one of them's alive, but he's heavy."

"Where were you coming from?" he asked the doctor in Russian.

"Wo shi yisheng . . . wo shi yisheng . . . ," the doctor repeated.

"He's totally out of it," said the other Chinese man. "Looks like his brains got frostbit."

Two more Chinese soon appeared. One of them held a sack of zoogenous canvas. He began to grab the nervous, neighing horses and put them in the bag.

"No mare?" asked the older man.

"No," the other answered him, and grinned as he pointed at the roan's croup sticking out of Crouper's coatsleeve. "Look where he crawled up!"

He grabbed the roan by his back legs and pulled him out of the sleeve. The roan neighed frantically.

"Talkative!" laughed the older man.

When all the horses were in the sack, the older Chinese nodded at the doctor:

"Pull him out."

Two of the others began to pull the doctor out of the hood. It wasn't easy: Platon Ilich's legs were wound around the corpse's legs, and his fur coat had frozen to the planks in the corner. The doctor realized that he was being saved.

"*Xie xie ni, xie xie ni*," he thanked the men in a hoarse croak, trying to help them with awkward movements.

It took the four of them to pull the doctor out of the sled. They set him down in the snow. The doctor tried to stand, leaning on the Chinese. But he immediately crumpled in the snow: his legs wouldn't obey. He couldn't feel them at all.

"*Xie xie ni, xie xie ni . . .* ," he kept on thanking them in a rasp as he wriggled in the deep snow.

The older Chinese man scratched his nose:

"Carry him to the train."

"Are we taking this one?" the young man asked, with a nod at Crouper.

"Xun, you know my stallion doesn't like dead people." The older one grinned, turning to look back with a half smile.

The man automatically looked in the direction the older man had indicated. There, about a hundred meters from the sled, stood a huge stallion, the height of a three-story building. A dappled gray, he was hitched up to a sleigh train carrying four wide cars: one green passenger car and three blue freight cars. The stallion was covered with a red blanket and stood with vapor snorting noisily from his incredibly wide nostrils. Crows circled above him and sat on his red back. The stallion's white mane was beautifully braided, and the steel rings on his harness sparkled in the sun.

Two more Chinese, wearing green uniforms, walked over from the train. Together, the four of them picked the doctor up and carried him.

"*Xie xie ni, xie xie ni* . . . ," the doctor rasped. He hadn't once moved his legs, which were numb and seemed utterly alien and useless.

He suddenly began to sob, realizing that Crouper had abandoned him forever, that he hadn't made it to Dolgoye, that he hadn't brought vaccine-2, and that in his life, the life of Platon Ilich Garin, it now appeared that a new phase was beginning, one that wouldn't be easy, would most likely be extremely difficult and grim, something he could never have imagined before.

"*Xie xie ni, xie xie n-n-ni* . . . ," the doctor cried, shaking his head, as though categorically disagreeing with everything that had happened and that was now taking place.

Tears streamed down his cheeks, grown thin and covered with stubble over the last few days. He clutched his pince-nez and kept shaking it, shaking and shaking, as though conducting some unseen orchestra of grief, crying and swaying in strong Chinese arms.

The older Chinese looked at Crouper. He lay alone in the emptied hood, looking as though he'd been placed in a grave that was too large for him. His gloved hands clutched his chest, as though holding and protecting his horses; one leg was tucked under, the other was turned out, frozen in an awkward position.

"Search him," the older Chinese commanded the younger.

The younger man reluctantly followed orders. A silver ruble, forty kopecks in copper, a lighter, and two crusts of bread were found in Crouper's coat pocket. He had no documents with him. The Chinese began to search under his cold clothes, and discovered two strings around his neck: one with a Russian Orthodox cross, the other, a key. It was the key to the stable. The Chinese tore off the key and handed it to his superior. The man turned the key around in his hand and tossed it in the snow.

"Cover him," the older man nodded.

The young man took the frost-stiffened matting, now hard as plywood, and covered the hood. The older man pointed at the sack with the horses and headed toward the train. The young Chinese picked up the sack, slung it over his back, and followed. The horses, already tossed about in the dark of the sack, had urinated on themselves and finally managed to calm down; now they just grunted and snorted. Only the restless roan gave a piercing neigh, bidding farewell to his master forever.